Zombie Princess Apocalypse

By
Jeffrey John Eyamie

PUBLISHED BY:
Woolly Mammoth Yarns
Winnipeg, Manitoba CANADA
www.zombieprincessapocalypse.com

Zombie Princess Apocalypse
Copyright © 2012 by Jeffrey John Eyamie
ISBN 978-0-9880088-2-3

This book is a work of fiction and any resemblance to persons, living or dead, or places, events or locales is purely coincidental. The characters are productions of the author's imagination and used fictitiously.

About The Author

Jeffrey John Eyamie wrote his first novel in Grade 3 and his second novel in journalism school. Thankfully, they are both locked away in hermetically sealed containers. A former child television star and grunge singer, Jeff once worked for Canada's minister of foreign affairs, conducted a feature interview with Bob Vila while sitting on the john, gave the commissioner of the National Hockey League a dressing-down on national television, and won second prize in a literary beauty contest. He now writes screenplays.

You can follow him on twitter: **@eyamie**

Thank You

First of all, thank you for taking the time to share this story with me. I know that having your time, attention and imagination for a little while is a huge privilege and I hope I don't squander it.

Thanks to all the people who helped turn Zombie Princess Apocalypse into this here novel: Jeff Solmundson, Lynn Dickinson, my mum Laurie Plumb, Zac Sanford, Gardner Grout, Nicole Jones, Orlanda Szabo and Clark Ransom. Each of these people is a fantastic writer in their own right. Check em out.

Thanks for the amazing artistic contribution, Tara Barker! Please check out www.tarabarker.net for portfolio pieces. Tara did the cover art as well as my amazing author photo.

Thanks to Sophie for giving me a reason to question power fantasies... especially the princess power fantasy.

And I saved the biggest thanks for last. Without my gorgeous, artistic, wise and gentle wife, Tiffany, I probably would have given up on my dream a long time ago. But since one dream of mine came true, now I know anything is possible.

xo Jeff

1

Once upon a time, about fourteen billion years ago, the universe was truly a *uni*verse. It was one unified object, the size of which was immeasurable. It could have been as large as the dot at the end of this sentence. It could have been infinite. Space didn't really exist, and neither did time, so there was no way to measure. The nothingness and somethingness existed in equal proportion at the same time. Before. These impossibilities were universal. I'm sure that these paradoxes would be stultifying to proletarian rabble such as yourselves, but you can't hear me anyway, so what's the difference?

At any rate, something happened. Some fourteen billion years after it happened, English-speaking scientists called it "the Big Bang," but really, the universe became the way we know it today when The Thing That Makes It So was born.

To create something that looks to us like an explosion the size of the cosmos itself, you need a lot of energy. Creative energy. Pure creative energy. Sure, an explosion big enough to commence existence (as humankind comprehends it) would look like a pretty scary little firecracker. But don't be afraid of it as you watch it split matter from antimatter; don't be afraid of it as you watch it unfurl galaxies like party favors from a dollar store; smile with pride in how you're connected to it as you watch the implosion of stars and the TNT sculpture of the planets formed from themselves. It's beautiful. It's creative. And none of it happens without the fire; without The Thing That Makes It So. Stuff needs to be shaped, and exploded, and heated up so it can be formed, and consumed so something new can be smithed from the embers. We humans are pretty chicken when it comes to fire. Since it can heat our skins up so well, we tend to fear it. Quite rightly so.

But think about this: when fire rolls through a forest, it creates more than it destroys. It rolls right through the forest, sucking up all the dried-out fuel and leaving behind something richer and more fertile, and where one dried-out birch may have stood, eaten into a husk by billions of beetles, four birches may grow in the blink of an eye – blink of an eye being about thirty years later. In the grand scheme of things, this is very efficient creativity.

The Thing That Makes It So isn't really comprised of that kind of fire, but that's about as close as we can get to comprehending The Thing without sounding thoroughly mystic. If I said to you: "the Devil! The Devil is the ultimate creative force in the universe because his fire creates! But not like you understand it, it's all metaphor so that we simple humans can understand!" Why, you'd probably reply, "Professor Pipsqueak, to the gallows with you!" Or "Professor Pipsqueak, you should talk to Jack Van Impe," or "Professor Pipsqueak, I will rouse a horde of social networking berserkers against you and you will be shamed into coming to your senses!" Oh yes. But – but if I just gently suggest to you that fire is The Thing That Makes It So, except this fire has a certain magnetism, especially when pooled into a volume much greater than our world can bear, then perhaps you can truly begin to understand how The Thing That Makes It So does its creative duty.

A) The Thing That Makes It So is fire.

Now let me truly blow your mind, as the kids say: what if fire had a consciousness? Well, I suppose if fire had a consciousness, it would be too terrifying to put your marsh mallows into it, eh? Ha! Ha!

If none of you are going to listen to me, I may as well amuse myself as I pontificate from this ridiculous trapeze. I find it mind-numbingly drab to swing on the trapeze like some kind of ape; at least I can keep my faculties well-engaged if I explain to you the nature of the universe and the creativity that threatens to destroy us and why I must participate in this debacle of a charade, pandering to your xenophobia so that you can feel comfortable in your own normal skins. Now where was I? What if fire had consciousness?

A) The Thing That Makes It So is fire.
B) The fire is conscious.

Well, if fire had consciousness, one would presume the fire had will, yes? Part right, but very astute of you to surmise. The Thing That Makes It So does indeed have a will; it does listen and act. But its will is not entirely free. No entity in the universe has truly free will. We have the freedom to think, but we cannot act without the blessing of our surroundings. We can dream of flapping our pinkie fingers and using the locomotion to fly us through the air, but gravity precludes it from becoming anything more than a fancy. And so it is with The Thing That Makes It So. It is a type of fire; a creative energy that appears quite destructive, and often destroys in order to create. And The Thing That Makes It So does indeed possess a sort of consciousness and will, but it is constrained by its connections. Just as man is connected to gravity, water, air, and the needs of survival, so too is The Thing That Makes It So connected to life and death. Mankind prides itself as a higher form of life, but The Thing That Makes It So sees humanity as the loudest form of life – the noisy neighbor whose bass-heavy disco music vibrates your wall, keeping you from sleep. And The Thing That Makes It So resents all that stridence, believe you me.

The Thing That Makes It So would be very happy to create something brand new from our immolation, like a green sapling rising from the cinders of an old, inflexible tree.

I believe, if the creative power of the universe had a wish, it would be to throw us all into the fire and start anew. Unfortunately for us all, the wishes of humanity are what shape the will of The Thing That Makes It So. Instead of starting anew, we are doomed to decline into a murk of our own creation. It's even worse.

Can you hear me over this preposterous carnival music, humanity? **The wishes of humanity shape the will of the Thing That Makes It So.**

Those wishes seem to be changing us in ways we can't comprehend.

A) The Thing That Makes It So is fire.
B) The fire is conscious.
C) We govern the fire with our wishes.

Is it truly beyond your comprehension? We can remedy that in three simple steps.

Step one: conceive of fire as creative.

Step two: conceive of fire with a consciousness.

Step three: conceive of fire that responds to the will of the universe.

Three simple steps and you would understand, if you could hear a word I'm saying.

We, as humans, seem to be rife with such egomania that we don't even consider ourselves connected to the universe. As though we were somehow above it! Laughable! We are so fabulously, spectacularly arrogant, aren't we? But the truth is -- and you can take it from me, Professor Pipsqueak -- the truth is that we are deeply and inextricably connected to the universe. And so we have as much say on the will of the universe as gravity does, or time, or any other force. If we worked together, and willed it, as one universal force, we could make anything possible, and The Thing That Makes It So would make it so. The fire would create it on our behalf.

I see you reading that Cosmopolitan magazine, young lady. That is not helpful.

Yes, I was talking to you. Did you hear anything else I said? Of course not. Do I look like a talking chimpanzee? I am Harvard-educated, you – unhand me, sir. The Browning's Traveling Oddities does not condone – halp!

—an unheard lecture from Professor Pipsqueak, recounted here verbatim.

2

Once upon a time, about eleven hundred years before the zombie princess apocalypse, a boy was adopted by a King. He was adopted in exchange for a modest bag of gold pieces. But the boy's parents, who operated a flour mill beside a rushing river, thought it to be destiny. After all, the boy bore the skin-markings of the blessed. He had never so much as coughed or spit up since he was born. When a fire ravaged the forest, their mill was the only structure untouched by the flame. So the millers thought the boy was meant to be adopted by the King and wished their baby well.

The King, as all Kings do, held ulterior motives. He had heard of the baby's prophetic skin markings. The oracles spoke of a prophecy that this boy, a simple miller's son, would someday marry the king's daughter. And the King was not prepared to allow his daughter's flower to be sullied by a commoner.

As they rode back to the castle, the King spied a deep river and ordered his caravan to halt. He had his newly-adopted son placed into a wooden box, had the box sealed with nails and wrapped in a leather satchel, then bound with four lashes and thrown into the river. It immediately sunk, pulled to the bottom by a relentless current. The King smiled to himself as he thought, 'bueno, my daughter is free from the fates.'

The caravan returned to the castle and the matter was promptly forgotten.

However, as luck would have it, the box was so well-sealed that the King's newly adopted and murdered son had plenty of air to breathe. The current pulled the box down, then the buoyancy created by the air-tightness popped it up to the surface of the river like a bubble, and that box-in-a-bag floated downstream, away from the backs of the King's caravan, around a couple of bends in the river, and right up against the millers' home. They were hardly surprised to see Luciano return and were hardly frugal in their spending of the King's gold.

Fourteen years later, the millers were among the aristocracy. Good fortune seemed to save its most blessed blessings for them. The skies were fair when they needed to be. Competitors met terrible fates. Flour had proven lucrative and the river had given them plenty of energy to create flour. Their boy was an adventurous lad who, like so many teens, thought himself to be immortal. He had ample evidence to support his hypothesis, too. One day, a rival suitor (the butcher's son), attempting to separate Luciano from the object of Luciano's affections, had stabbed at Luciano with a stone meat cleaver the butcher used to cleave cattle in two. But the cleaver wasn't fastened to its handle well, and when the jealous boy cocked back to throw the cleaver, the stone slid off the wood and split his skull.

A week later, when Luciano was caught with a neighboring farmer's daughter in the barn, the farmer saw Luciano's silhouette and thought it to be the concussed butcher's son, who was as lecherous as Luciano. Luciano escaped with the help of the farmer's daughter, the farmer went to town, found the other boy and slapped his head, which was enough to re-open his old wound and kill him. As the constabulary held the farmer in custody, Luciano was able to spend plenty of time with the farmer's daughter. Such was the good fortune of the millers' son, Luciano, until the King passed through their town on his way to a wolf hunt.

Angrily, the King accused the millers of subterfuge, but the millers merely told the King what had happened: the boy was a foundling who floated up to their wheel in a wooden box. The King knew the truth, but could not speak it. The millers knew it as well, since the boy was quite unique in his appearance, what with the prophetic markings and red hair. But they continued with the charade, the King congratulating them on their fortunes.

The next morning, as the King embarked on his hunt, he handed the millers a letter and requested their boy hand-deliver the King's letter to the Queen. The millers, knowing Luciano's prophecy to marry the King's daughter, excitedly sent for him at once.

The letter instructed the Queen to have Luciano beheaded forthwith and without mercy, for he was the boy destined to soil their daughter's virtue.

Luciano bounded down the road, the letter not even sealed completely. He had no care for what the letter said. He assumed he was about to meet his wife, and in Luciano's imagination, the Princess would be the fairest young lady in the land. In his pocket, Luciano fumbled with the ring he had hidden away for years -- the ring his parents had given to him for his proposal to the Princess, as the markings on his skin had foretold. The ring was Lucky's most prized possession. He couldn't wait to shackle his wife with it.

But he didn't meet his wife. He got lost in the forest and stumbled upon an old shanty shack. Inside the shack, a gnarled-up old crone with a banana-shaped nose rocked in a rocking chair. She warned Luciano that he had just broken into the home of a thieves' guild, and the crone said they would kill him as soon as they returned. Luciano went for a nap and waited. It was the first time in his life that Luciano had become bored with being impossible to kill.

Once Luciano was asleep, the crone spied his letter and reached for it. Luciano was a deep sleeper, since nothing could make him afraid, and so withdrawing the letter from his pocket was simple enough. She noticed the marking on Luciano's wrist. It made her curious. She unbuttoned Luciano's collar and spied the marking on his breastbone; she lifted his pantleg and saw the marking on his calf. The banana-nosed old woman then read the letter and cackled, and when the six thieves arrived home from their night of plundering, they set about giving the King a proper what-for.

But something happened to Luciano in his dreams. A figure appeared to him; red and fiery and frightening. Luciano assumed it was the Devil himself. The Devil told Luciano that his destiny would force him to marry the King's daughter, and the thing that made him how he was would keep him immortal only until the day he wed the Princess. On that day, the thing that made him how he was would have no further use for him, and he would become common. The Devil laughed, for he knew Luciano had grown to be a young man without ever learning to fear or avoid danger or be cautious. The Devil knew Luciano would surely die.

In his dream, Luciano asked the Devil what to do.

The Devil's expression soured, as though he did not like the question. But the Devil answered, nonetheless:

"I am your servant. Your wish is my command."

And with that, Luciano had acquired knowledge no boy had been lucky enough to acquire, before or since. He had become an agent of The Thing That Makes It So. But he was a double-agent.

He engineered a plan to send the princess to eternal damnation, where she could never be married, and Luciano could live forever. The plan resulted in Luciano plucking three golden hairs from the Devil himself, sending the King to ferry the dead across the river into Hell, and Luciano narrowly escaping the clutches of the Princess by riding a rotten log across the ocean to a world no one knew existed yet.

3

Once upon a time, about sixteen years before the zombie princess apocalypse, a girl was born. She was born in the snow, in an igloo where night was perpetual, and she was beautiful. Her name was Emily Dillinger, but she was immediately called Emm, and her parents were so happy to have her that her Dad whooped a big whoop when he saw ten fingers and ten toes come out. He saw Mom was okay jumped up and down with such fervor that he hit his head on the top of the igloo. Sculpted snow fell over the place. The Inuit who helped them covered their faces with big mitts, bashful as they snickered at him. But Emm's Dad didn't care. He covered himself in the snow and straw, kicked it up all over the place, as he danced a jig for all of them. It was the greatest day in his life. Magical day.

Emm had no way of knowing this, but Mrs. Dillinger cried tears that were not one hundred percent tears of joy. For Mrs. Dillinger had seen a vision, long ago, and the vision continued to become reality. It was a new dawn, a new day, and a new year, and Mrs. Dillinger knew it would be the last year of her life. As she tearfully stared into the gorgeous face of her new baby Emm, Daphne Dillinger vowed to soak up every last moment of joy in this final year. She vowed to protect Emm with every fiber of her being. She tried to record all of it in her mind, to take it with her to wherever she was going. Mr. Dillinger smiled his usual, disarming smile as he wiped the tears away from her eyes. He held baby Emm, who wasn't much bigger than the palm of his hand, and their Inuit hosts wrapped Emm in a papoose. Mrs. Dillinger knew it was time to tell her husband the truth.

And so, as Emm had her first sleep in the middle of the perpetual night, where the sun didn't shine for days on end, Mrs. Dillinger told Mr. Dillinger about her dreams. As she rested her head in his lap, and Derek Dillinger ran his fingers through her shimmering black hair, she narrated her dream of how a terrible woman had visited The Thing That Makes It So. The woman had a wish, and the wish was for the Dillingers to be scorched by the fires of The Thing, and for their baby to lead humanity into the fire of creation itself, to give rise to a new age, where humanity used its power over The Thing to shape the universe as humankind saw fit. Which happened to mean the same thing as saying that The Thing That Makes It So would shape the universe as the terrible woman saw fit. It was a stylish shape. A shape where everyone was fashionable and stylish and lived out their fantasies and got their wishes granted, just like a fairy tale.

Mr. and Mrs. Dillinger concocted a plan. Then, as the perpetual night began to surrender to the sun's rays, they gathered the rest of Browning's Traveling Oddities, boarded a train headed south, entertained folks with their prestidigitation and fortune-telling, and never stayed in the same place for more than a week.

But they couldn't outrun The Thing That Makes It So, and its new apostle, forever.

4

Once upon a time, about ten years before the zombie princess apocalypse, a caravan of crappy-looking old minivans came to a stop at the side of a desert highway. The minivan at the front spewed some kind of vapor into the air, a mixture of steam and smoke and burning radiator fluid. It stunk.

That's why Pedro growled a little when he lifted the hood. He didn't normally growl. That was really just a stereotype, that wolf boys and wolf girls growled. Pedro was just playing to that stereotype during the show, when he would growl and bay at the moon and show off his agility by climbing tree-shaped poles. No, wolf people were just very hairy people with a genetic anomaly given the name hypertrichosis by doctors.

Pedro gave people what they expected and it paid the bills. Nobody asked Pedro, or any other member of Browning's Traveling Oddities, any questions about who they were or what they were doing. Which was kind of the point.

Pedro the Wolf-Boy growled at the stink of the engine and then walked over to the driver's side window, where his boss sat, smiling.

"Water-pump, Señior Dillinger," Pedro told him.

Señior Dillinger, whom the rest of the world called The Amazing Dillinger, nodded.

"Grab Professor Pipsqueak," The Amazing Dillinger said, "Track us down a tow truck. And some dinner."

Pedro the Wolf-Boy stroked his facial fur and smiled. "Bring Professor Pipsqueak to town? Are you sure that's a good idea? We don't want to scare the townsfolk." They both knew Pedro the Wolf-Boy's wolfen features, which covered all of his body and included an embouchure that suggested he had fangs (although he didn't really – they were just very prominent eyeteeth. It was kind of a stereotype, that wolf-boys had fangs.)

They shared a warm smile and a knowing eyeball-twinkle at Professor Pipsqueak's expense. It was the kind of look that a boss could share with an employee if they were boss and employee for decades. Or if they had saved the world together a few times.

"Right," Dillinger said. "You better do the talking when you get to town, then." They continued to share the smile as Pedro left Dillinger's side with a "Si, Señior."

In the passenger seat, holding The Amazing Dillinger's hand, Steph Dillinger turned to the back of the van. The red desert air gave Steph's skin a golden tint and tinged her blonde hair. Derek Dillinger looked over at her and thought Steph couldn't get more beautiful than she was at this very moment, a light glisten of sweat made her glimmer like a desert jewel.

"Emm, do you need to pee?" she said as she turned.

Emm, six years old, hair of coal, skin of snow, nodded sheepishly at her.

"Come on," Steph undid her seatbelt.

But a strange feeling came over The Amazing Dillinger. An ominous urge to get out of the van and have a talk with Emm. And say some words that he hoped would not be his last. The feeling in his throat and stomach got worse quickly and the hope became fear and the fear became knowledge. The Amazing Derek Dillinger knew that he was about to die.

"Wait," Derek said. "I'll take her." He tried to mask his horrible feeling but he could hear the lilt in his own voice betray him. Steph didn't seem to notice, though. She got out of the van, pulled the wheelchair out from the back, unfolded it at the driver's side door, and helped The Amazing Dillinger into his wheelchair. Derek put on his black fedora while Steph put a roll of toilet paper in his lap.

"Are you sure about this? It's pretty sandy, Derek. And hot."

"Don't worry, pretty lady. We'll be fine." He pulled at the brim of his fedora and smiled at Steph, for what he hoped would not be the last time. "Give us a kiss."

Dutifully, she did, then stretched like a cat as Emm and her father went into the desert, where no living thing could escape the sun.

They got about a hundred yards away from the highway before Emm found a spot in amongst the bushes to do her business. Derek squinted a curse at the sun, his dress shirt soaked with sweat.

"Daddy," Emm said she waddled out from behind some scrub.

"Ya." Getting that one syllable out of his throat was exhausting.

"Can you teach me the magic?" Emm leaned on his armrest, nearly close enough to kiss. Derek pulled himself together and tried to bring his sun-addled vision into focus. *One last time, for Emm.*

"Like this stuff?" Dillinger mustered a big magician's flourish, because that stuff always came easier than breathing to The Amazing Dillinger, particularly so at this moment. After the big flourish, a necklace with an opal heart pendant dangled from Derek's fingers. Emm, in joyful shock, clutched her chest where the pendant should have been.

"It's not really magic, love..." Derek wheezed.

Emm lowered her head so Derek could put the necklace back on her. Derek continued to wheeze, his fingers barely able to bring the necklace over her head. Emm didn't notice her father's distress. "So magic is fake?" she asked.

To Derek, the sun felt like it was getting closer and closer. And that made him angry. He could feel the life slipping away from him. *Not yet.*

"Magic isn't an illusion or trick... magic is energy... alive in us... connecting us..."

"So how come I can't fly then?"

A grimace overpowered Derek's feeble attempt to smile. "Doesn't work that way... every... everything... under the sun –" And with that, The Amazing Dillinger, whom his wife called Derek, toppled into the desert sand from the lofty heights of his wheelchair, and clutched his heart as it exploded.

"Stepmom," he gurgled. Emm screamed for Steph and fell to her knees, cradling her father's head in her tiny six-year-old arms, which shivered in desert heat. Derek tried to swallow back the blood and bile that urged itself up and out of his throat.

"What's wrong? What's wrong? Daddy!"

Derek wanted to wipe Emm's tears away, but there was no time. "Listen to me. The universe wills it and it is so... people don't realize they are connected to *all* of it..." *It's not coming out right*, Derek thought. *Not enough time.*

Tears covered Emm's face as she wailed. Steph arrived in time to see Derek's grimace turn to a smile of final relief.

"Got all I wished for. I had everything." He said to Steph, looking up to her face one last time. *I'm coming, Daphne.*

"Not yet!" Steph roared at the sun.

"Don't die, Daddy, don't die," was all Emm could say as she watched her father let go. All Derek could do was whisper "Never forget... who we are..." to Emm before his final breath escaped his lungs and climbed up to the red desert sun, above Emm and her stepmother, above Browning's Traveling Oddities, and out of this world.

And that's how Emm Dillinger, the world's last hope against the zombie princess apocalypse, became an orphan.

5

"Ladies and Gentlemen, the Devastating Dillingers of Doom! Give them a big round of applause. What a great show!"

Two people clapped. That was two-thirds of all the people in the tent and two of the three spectators seemed to be in a rush to get out of there. Emm was too. She turned and walked away as Steph unbuckled herself, hoping to get a solid hour of alone time before the next show. Maybe listen to some tunage on her discman and read a book the bearded lady had lent her.

As Emm slipped a robe over her shoulders, covering up the sequined leotard that sparkled all teal and sparkly and so not like Emm at all, a man walked up to her. Emm paid no attention to the man until he touched Emm's elbow.

"Nice show," the man said. Emm pulled her elbow away and tied up her robe. This wasn't the first time someone thought they could talk to her just because she worked the sideshow, but this guy was particularly gross. He was big and sweaty and hairy and extra disgusting. He had an odor about him that was kind of metallic, but also like rotten egg. It made Emm afraid.

"Why don't the two of you come to my place for a sweet tea... I'm just outside of town." That got Emm's attention, but she pretended it didn't. She yanked off her ballet slippers and plunked her feet into some leather Doc Martens, rushing to get out of there.

"Come on," the guy said. "How much for the two of you?" he said. And that's all he got to say.

Steph didn't even offer a threat. She just cold-cocked him with a left cross that probably popped his mandible bone off its joint. His sweat made a spray as he spun into the ground. Steph grabbed Emm's hand and headed out of the sideshow tent.

Ziggy the Zookeeper burst into the tent. He was like all the other sideshow bosses, Emm thought. Weird, weird, weird. And sad. Ziggy looked at the floor and looked up at Steph. "Don't you know who that is?"

"I don't care if he's a flying pig. He's still a pig."

"That there's the man owns the biggest chain of GM dealerships in the state. You don't punch a guy with money like that. He says jump, you jump."

"He was treating us like property."

"You are property. You're my property. You do what I say. You don't like it, you can take your no-talent kid and start hitching out of this podunk town."

Steph hadn't unmade her fist yet and when Ziggy said "no-talent kid," he nearly tasted it. Instead she got under his chin and urged him to call her kid no-talent one more time. The disgusting GM dealership guy started to wake up. Ziggy said nothing, but he took a step back.

Steph harrumphed and took Emm to the carnies' trailer, where they had stored all their worldly possessions. Steph masked her tears as she lugged Emm to the trailer, but Emm could see the shiny streaks on the side of Steph's face. Emm imagined Steph must have been as grossed out by the disgusting smelly man as Emm was.

The other carnies' kids – several of whom were older than twelve-year-old Emm – were standing around the trailer tossing a football when Emm and Steph marched past. A thirteen-year-old girl caught the football absently and gave Emm the stinkeye. Emm didn't even know the girl's name, but Emm knew they all hated her and this girl was the ringleader.

Emm was the only one who had to work. The only one who had to pull on a teal sequined leotard that sparkled in sun, and the other kids – kids of freaks – thought Emm was the biggest freak of all. "Nice tutu," the girl said to her, to which Emm could find no witty reply, since Emm also hated it. "It's a leotard," was all Emm could find in response, and she delivered it with as much venom as possible. Emm pulled her hand away from Steph's. Steph was too ashamed from crying to show her face to the other carnies' kids, so she kept on going, offering a warbling "I'll get us packed" before leaving Emm alone, in the dirt outside the crew's trailer, with eight nasty carny kids. Emm didn't know any of their names, and they didn't know hers, but they despised her just the same.

The girl who said "nice leotard" threw the football at Emm, who had never caught a football in her life. Emm put a hand out to catch it, but the strange shape made it bounce off her hand and into her face, taking a layer of makeup with it.

The thirteen-year-old girl stomped her way up to Emm, ready to fight, but Emm would never do such a thing. There was no fight in Emm. When the other kids got closer and threatened to gang up on her, Emm backed away.

Emm started to ball herself up before she even realized she was doing it. She murmured "this sideshow sucks anyway" as they got closer and closer. *I want to fly away or melt into the ground or evaporate into nothingness,* Emm thought to herself. *I don't want to be this anymore.*

"This sideshow sucks 'cause you're in it, twinkle-toes," the girl said to Emm. Then Emm got shoved in three different directions, bounced from bully to bully. *Even the freak kids think I'm a reject.*

And then a nine-year-old boy punched Emm in the breadbasket, and the girl who razzed her clawed at her robe until it was halfway down Emm's back, like a straightjacket, and then all the kids got in on the fun, punching and scratching out the sequins and knocking Emm to the dirt, where she turtled to no avail. The kicks winded her, made it impossible to breathe; she felt a hot rivulet of blood dripping from behind her nose and into her throat.

"Think you're a big star," the lead bully murmured as Emm started to lose consciousness. *Take me away from all of this. Give me a school uniform and pigtails and Barbie dolls and a room of my own. Give me a house with a kitchen that can cook food and a backyard with a tree in it. I don't want to be a weirdo. I want my Daddy.*

Steph came out of the trailer and the kids scurried off, but Emm wasn't conscious for any of it. When she finally came to, Emm and Steph were on a bus bound for Arkansas, and another sideshow gig Steph had lined up through some old friends. Emm cried into her torn-up leotard for hours. She begged Steph to quit, but Steph said they had a job to do, and that someday it would all make sense and someday, Emm would actually be glad she was what she was.

Emm didn't believe it

6

Wounds became scars and scars became calluses. Despite her efforts to disguise it, Emm had blossomed into a head turning sixteen-year-old, with hair as black as pitch, lips as red as oxblood, and skin of the finest porcelain. Not that Emm ever noticed, but it was common for boys to glance her way, think to themselves, "oh man, that is a pretty face hiding behind those gloomy black rags and crappy emo haircut," and mean it as a compliment. Emm was oblivious to that kind of thing.

When they had lived on the road, wandering from sideshow to sideshow like nomads, Emm was oblivious to people who liked her, because she got so agitated when she was around other people that she had a hard time doing anything but vibrating a little. When they were on the road, working the sideshows, just walking through a truck stop's diner was an exercise in trying not to vibrate, what with all the commotion and lewd looks and truckers.

Now they were in the city of Modesta, California, and just being in one place for two weeks was starting to make Emm vibrate in her sleep. Maybe she should have been excited to have a kitchen to cook food, her own room with a bed that held up a mattress with coils in it, and a back yard where she could practice, but scars had become calluses. Maybe the little girl that Emm used to be might have enjoyed their new home. Emm was a carny, humiliating though that truth may be. She just tried not to vibrate.

Since they had moved to Modesta, into a little bungalow that Steph said some old friends had offered them to live in rent-free, Emm had looked at her feet a lot to try not to vibrate. The sleepy bedroom community of Modesta was barely even a city, but it was too big for Emm. Everybody had a dream here and everybody was here to chase it. There were no carny folk. No weirdoes. There weren't even other kids on her block, just people with Volvos and Beemers and brand new suits and mansions that dwarfed the bungalow they lived in. Everyone got up at six o'clock, walked out of their McMansions with a thermal mug of coffee in their hands, talking into their wireless earpiece thingamajiggies, got into their black import car and sped off to the freeway, in pursuit of the dream they were already living. Modesta was nothing but cookie cutter mansions, one high school, one park, two hills, and one shopping mall. Anybody who worked in Modesta, who serviced the extravagant Modestans, seemed to have been imported from some other town.

Everybody who lived in Modesta headed for the freeway at six o'clock in the morning, living the dream.

Everybody except Emm.

Emm's dream was to be a regular kid. That's what she was thinking about as she wiped the sweat from her eyes, midway through morning practice in her new back yard. *What's it like to just be completely, utterly, invisibly average?* Then she thought about how not-invisible it would be to start at her new school in the middle of the final semester.

"Tell me again why can't I just start next year?" Emm asked Steph. Emm sucked up a big gulp of air and threw another hatchet. "What if they hate me?"

"What's not to love?" Steph said. A hatchet landed two inches from Steph's orbital bone. She glanced over at it and glowered back at Emm. "Don't be smart." Steph spun lazily on a human-sized wheel across the yard from Emm. Small silvery hatchets dotted the wheel. They had been at this for a while.

Emm stretched her arm like a baseball pitcher doing warmups.

"Seriously," Emm said, "as if I have to do a speech on my first day." Emm gathered up her best dumb-person voice to ape, "'Nice speech, orphan side show freak'."

"You're being ridiculous," Steph said from the wheel. "You're going to hit the ground running."

Then Emm started in on another set of reps as Steph continued:

"Just be you." Thunk. "They'll love you." Thunk. "Don't want to tell them about the carny stuff?" Thunk. "They don't need to know." Thunk. "I'm sure it'll be just like Glee, honey."

Emm grabbed a water bottle and plopped down on a lawn chair.

"If the misfits have to sing at this school, just kill me now."

Steph, expert sideshow assistant that she was, leapt from the spinning wheel like a swan. She sat down in a lawnchair beside Emm and swiped Emm's water bottle to take a swig. Being a human hatchet target was hard work in the California sun. Steph put a hand on Emm's knee. "Life is tough enough when you're out of school. Just take the time to enjoy being normal."

"How do I do that?"

"Blend."

"How do you blend with cream when you're a lemon like me? I'll just curdle everything."

"Make lemonade, or some parental cliché like that, right? Listen: sometimes you gotta suck some lemons to get to the lemon meringue pie. Okay?"

"What does that even mean?"

"That means you can do anything, even if it sucks for a while."

Emm grabbed a towel and buried her face in it. "Mmmmf, this is already stressing me out." She felt the vibratey feeling coming back.

Steph reddened. "Hey. Try working double shifts while being a mom and dad and homeschool teacher, all at the same time, then talk to me about stress."

Emm pulled her face out of the towel, surprised at the anger. She looked over at her stepmother sourly. Steph tried blowing some frustration into the air.

"Just go, blend, get the first day overwith," Steph said. "Make some friends."

Yeah, right. "Friends…"

"One. Friend."

Steph got up and scuffled Emm's hair, proclaimed "dibs on the shower," and slipped inside. Emm stared out at the spinning wheel, scarred with a dozen hatchets, and wondered if she'd ever feel at home without a hatchet in her hand and a barker outside the tent. She wondered what was wrong with her.

Steph popped her head back out of the door.

"You got your homework done, right?"

7

Sprawled out at the edge of sleepy Modesta, just past a couple of breast-shaped hills and a Carl's Jr., Jacob Williams High School was your typical giant bedroom community high school. It was like a massive brick roach motel, if the roaches wore designer dresses and tied sweaters around their necks. Emm would have thought 'oh man, this is worse than 90210' if she had ever watched TV before three days ago, when she and Steph watched an episode of Glee. Emm thought TV was the biggest waste of time she had ever encountered and vowed to make her one hour of Glee-watching the only hour of TV she would ever watch in her life.

Emm did listen to music, though, lots of music on her discman, so she knew exactly what the banner over the front doors meant: "THRILLER PROM! GET YOUR TIX." Her top-of-the-line home schooling taught her that "tix" meant tickets. Emm made a mental note to avoid buying tix at all costs.

She vibrated a little as she pushed on the front door. Without noticing it, Emm looked at her black jeans and Misfits t-shirt and told herself *I will never fit in here, ever.* Those kind of thoughts were just automatic.

The students who bothered to even look in Emm's direction weren't much help as she asked for Mr. Blake's office. Most of them just laughed, like asking for Mr. Blake was some kind of joke. All the students were taller than Emm. And prettier than Emm (or so Emm thought). They certainly had more expensive clothes than Emm. After feeling like a salmon swimming upstream for a couple of minutes, she finally saw his door: Mr. Blake. Guidance Counselor.

Emm expected Mr. Blake to look a certain way; the way all guidance counselors looked in Emm's imagination: lab coat, pen protector, thick black glasses, beard. British accent. Pipe. Leathery skin. Six feet tall. "I have a group of friends all picked out for you," the guidance counselor would say. Yep, that's what she imagined.

She got the leathery skin right. The rest... not so much. Mr. Blake wore a tweed blazer which threatened to split at the shoulders, he was so thick. No beard, but a well-waxed moustache. No lab coat. No pen protector. His office was hidden by mountains of paperwork. And so was Mr. Blake. For Mr. Blake was a little person, barely visible behind his file folder mountains.

"It says here, Miss Dillinger, that you have been home schooled to a sophomore level?" the voice said from behind the folders.

Emm peeked around the paperwork to get a glimpse of Mr. Blake, who looked immersed in her file.

"Sort of... I mean we didn't have a home till we moved here, so it was homeless home schooling." She took a seat and couldn't see him anymore.

"Didn't have a home? Were you some kind of model? Traveling salesman?"

"What? No... we were performers. Uh, Traveling

entertainers I guess. I don't really want to talk about it."

"I see. It's just – you have model features. Despite your attempts to hide them, you are quite lovely," said the file folder mountain Mr. Blake was hiding behind. He attempted to change the subject. "It's unusual to enrol so late...."

"Not my choice."

"Choices. I see many girls who are ready to make very bad choices, just to be one of the many... choices that sometimes scar them for life."

"What, like botox? Butt implants? You hear about those fix-a-flat people who injected concrete into their butts? How stupid is that?"

"I had not."

"You should google it. It looks like there's a tire in their pants. Anyway..."

"Anyway... my counsel to you is to rise above the crowd, Miss Dillinger. If you ever need guidance... my door is open."

It wasn't a pre-chosen circle of friends, but Mr. Blake's offer made Emm feel genuinely better. "Thanks," Emm said, just as the school rang.

"That would be the bell, which indicates that you are presently late for... Earth Sciences."

Emm jumped up and spun for the door. A pang of anxiety shot through her gut as she remembered the speech she needed to make. "Thanks," she offered.

"My door is open," he said again.

Emm stood there, peering through the file folders into Mr. Blake's eyes. *Maybe Mr. Blake is the one friend I'll make today.* She smiled at him.

"My door is open. Walk through it." *Oh. He meant that literally.* Emm headed for class.

As soon as she was gone, Mr. Blake reached for his phone and hit number one on the speed-dial. "She's a dead ringer for Snow White, isn't she?" he told the phone. "I thought it best to give her some time before she gets the key."

That made the voice on the phone angry.

"She needs time to adjust!" Mr. Blake barked.

The voice barked back.

"Well, let's just see how she fares," Blake blustered.

8

Mr. Hinkley was in mid-speech when Emm slipped into the back of the classroom. "Climate Change" was scrawled in huge letters on the chalkboard.

Emm had an expectation of what a science teacher would look like, too, and this time, Mr. Hinkley did not disappoint: corduroy blazer replete with leather elbow patches, bald toilet-seat-shaped hairdo, matching corduroy pants. Mr. Hinkley looked like a pile of leaves. Orange and brown and ready to get jumped all over. He glanced over at Emm and decided not to say anything as she snuck into class, her butterflies now metamorphosing into dragonflies, and the dragonflies metamorphosing into dragons.

"Hopefully you've all reviewed An Inconvenient Truth," he droned in a nasal monotone, "which clearly demonstrated blah blah blah…" Emm tuned him out and made her way to an open seat, busily examining all of the other students who surrounded her now like sharks. They weren't paying attention to the teacher either. There were a lot of preppy girls in this class, but one girl seemed to sit a little taller, be a little blonder. A little more perfect. The blonde girl had the longest, Barbiest hair, not like Steph's blonde at all. Steph's hair was bleached by the sun. This All-American Barbie literally wore red, white and blue like she was a star on Old Glory itself. She stared into space with the bluest, emptiest, most vacant eyes. Whatever was on going on in her brain, Emm decided, it wasn't going on in this dimension.

There were two size-fourteen feet luxuriating on the blonde girl's desk. Feet belonging to the enormous dude sitting in the desk beside her's. The guy was obviously a football or basketball or rugby or mixed martial arts player with his fancy leather letterman's jacket. He reclined, sideways, in his desk, staring at the wall, totally ignoring Mr. Hinkley. The other kids secretly ignored Mr. Hinkley. These two were doing it like it was a competition. They both chewed gum.

As Emm sat down, she squeaked her chair a little. It silenced Mr. Hinkley. Everyone turned to gawk at her.

"I'd say she's fashionably late," the blondest girl said, "but look at her. Nothing fashionable about that." All of her sycophants snickered in unison.

One kid – a boy, very slight, with coke bottle eyeglasses and a Frank Frazetta t-shirt, barked at the blondest girl from the back of the class. "At least give her a day to acclimatize before you unleash full Jessica on her," he said.

"Suck it, Sperm," was Jessica's reply.

"Such a clever retort. Sperm must be something you're very familiar with."

Letterman Jacket made a fist at Olly.

Mr. Hinkley jumped in. "Very well, class. A savvy orator knows when he is about to lose his audience. Olly, the podium is yours."

The boy with the coke bottle glasses and half-naked lady on a dragon shirt shuffled his way up to the front. As he passed Emm's desk, he leaned in a little.

"Just ignore her," Olly said, loud enough for the preppies to hear it. "The only thing she's missing is the tiara."

The big guy pointed a meaty finger at Olly. "Watch it," the big guy mouthed. Olly grabbed a remote from the podium and clicked. A power point presentation lit up behind him.

"Power point," Emm muttered to herself, feeling just a little more inferior.

The title slide:

THE END OF DAYS
By Oliver Ford

Olly began ominously: "Global warming. Is the end of the world coming? I say yes. So does the Center for Disease Control."

He clicked the remote and power point moved to a screen capture of the CDC's Zombie Apocalypse social media campaign page: blogs.cdc.gov/publichealthmatters/2011/05/preparedness-101-zombie-apocalypse.

"Are you kidding me?" Jessica said.

"Prepare for global warming," Olly said, unabated. The next slide showed an image of sunscreen. "Not that hard to prepare for global warming. But Al Gore says this is our biggest threat." Another click and the class was treated to a pencil-crayon drawing of the sun, while pencil-crayon stick figures burned to death on the ground.

The class groaned.

"Prepare for the zombie apocalypse," Olly said. The next slide showed a zombie survival kit, a photo obviously taken by Olly, complete with backpack, flashlights, canned food, water bottle, radio, candles, a hammer, a metal spike, an aerosol can, a barbecue lighter and a skateboard helmet.

The preppies verged on an all-out class rebellion.

"I don't know about you," Olly said over the din, "But I'm a little more worried about this."

The gory photo of a movie zombie eating its prey makes the class grimace. Olly smiled at the class, proudly. He seemed almost pleased by the chaos he had created. Emm smiled to herself.

"Are you seriously serious?" Jessica said.

"When the zombies come, you'll thank me."

"You so need help, little Sperm."

"Do I, Jessica?" The class became silent as Olly challenged Jessica. "Am I the one who needs help? Let me ask you this: what do zombies look like?"

"Olly..." Mr. Hinkley warned.

"Your parents?" Jessica said. Her followers snickered.

"What if zombies aren't like the movies? What if they don't eat brains? What if they're just close-minded idiots with poor communication skills and bad skin?"

Jessica furtively touched her cheek.

Mr. Hinkley broke in. "Not cool, Olly," he said. "No ad hominem attacks. Also zombies have nothing to do with global warming. Or reality."

"But – "

Mr. Hinkley gave Olly the 'sit-down' gesture with

his hand. After a second, Olly realized there was no winning and left the podium. Letterman Jacket gave Olly a shove that forced Olly clanging into the desks. Olly shuffled back to his desk as the popular kids scowled at him.

"Now, Emily Dillinger," Mr. Hinkley said, "welcome to our little kabuki theatre. Please regale us with your worldly wisdom on the topic of climate change."

The dragons in her stomach all simultaneously breathed fire into her intestines. This was it. Once, Emm got to perform her hatchet-throwing in front of three hundred people all at once. That was way easier than this. Emm took a deep, deep breath. The deepest she could muster. She stood up with some papers sloppily stacked in her hand.

"I don't have any Power Point slide things," she said.

"Visual aids are for bonus points," Mr. Hinkley replied, not that gently. "Bonus points you could have sorely used, I'm sure, but try not to worry."

Jessica whispered something to the other preppie girls and Emm knew right away that it was a joke Jessica was telling – a joke about Emm. Emm thought about that nine-year-old carny kid who punched her in gut. The room was getting hot and she couldn't quite see straight. But Emm put her papers down on the podium, tried to stop vibrating, and began to read.

"From the beginning of time, humans have asked the sun for mercy, for fertility, for just about anything. Why?"

A cricket would have had the good sense to keep quiet, even though it would have been heard loud and clear. Emm wasn't sure they understood what she was trying to say, so she said it in another way: "Why do we ask the sun to give us anything?"

Still less than crickets. "Today, sunspot activity is cycling downward, throwing us into global *cooling* for the next several decades."

An audible "what?!" came from a girl wearing hemp necklaces and beaded braids. The girl looked like the kind of girl who felt she knew everything about Mother Earth.

On the words "global cooling," Mr. Hinkley stopped writing notes at his desk and shot Emm a look. It was not an encouraging look. He slowly shook his head and mouthed "not cool." This made Emm hurry a little, and that was a good thing. She started to forget what she was doing and pass along the information.

"Doctor Raymond Wheeler of the University of Kansas discovered that humanity is linked to the warming and cooling trends of the sun. Our dark ages, our bloodiest wars – our lowest points as a civilization? They all happen during the cold times."

"Whatevs," Jessica said, pulling out her smartphone.

And with that snide comment, all the momentum was gone. Emm's eyes were drawn to Jessica and her stupid smartphone. *It's not working*, Emm thought. Emm had worked really hard on this presentation and it was bombing. All the googling, all the study; connecting dots from her findings like the unraveling of a great mystery. It didn't matter to any of them. Half-heartedly, she kept going.

"So next time, you wish upon a star, maybe wish on the star that's closest to us. If enough of us wish at the same time…"

Letterman Jacket made a 'cuckoo' whistle and swirled his finger. That got a big laugh.

"…maybe we can get the global warming we need."

Mr. Hinkley needed to rise to keep the class from exploding. Emm looked over to him, desperate for help. He didn't offer her any.

"No, really..." she pleaded, "wishing on our star works... in 1979 – Skylab – a group meditation reduced solar activity long enough to save a satellite from crashing into Australia. It's **real!**"

"And that, class... CLASS!" Mr. Hinkley boomed his voice and everyone froze. "That, class, is why we don't endorse home schooling."

Emm had a choice to make. She could either give up, go home, run from this chance with her tail between her legs... or she could stand up for herself. She had the sudden urge to throw hatchets.

"Google it, Mr. Hinkley," she growled. "It happened."

"I just googled you," Jessica said. "The Devastating Dillingers of Doom?"

They knew. They found out. Emm's instincts quickly flipped from fight to flight. Steph had shown Emm the internet in libraries all over America, but Emm had no idea that *she* was on there, too. The preppie kids weren't done.

"What else does it say," Letterman Jacket said.

"A hatchet thrower – aww, your Dad died."

"Not cool, Jessica," Mr. Hinkley feebly warned.

"Daddy issues. That so explains the haircut." The preppies laughed.

Emm bolted without looking back. It was all over for her at Jacob Williams High School. All this buildup, a speech she thought would knock them dead, the wish to be normal she had harbored since she was a little girl with no mom and no dad and no home. It all went up in smoke in that instant.

Emm wished she were dead.

There was a moment of silence in the classroom after Emm left it. No one was quite sure what to do and Mr. Hinkley wasn't offering any leadership. He looked down at his notes and scribbled something beside Emm's name. An F, no doubt.

"Lily Farquhuar," Hinkley announced, and the granola girl with the hemp necklaces and beaded braids rose to speak. And Emm was forgotten by Mr. Hinkley's Earth Sciences class.

Except for Olly.

Olly swiped his arm across his desk, sending his books to the floor. He shot up to his feet. With a glare at Letterman Jacket, and then a glare at Mr. Hinkley, Olly stormed out. "You people are idiots," Olly muttered.

"Not cool, Olly," Mr. Hinkley called at Olly's back, like it would have done anything.

9

It was a moment you would see in just about any melodrama. Emm covered her face with her hands, blubber-snot coating her palms, as she flailed her way into the hallway. First day – first *hour* – at school and Emm was already running away. At least school would teach Emm a little lesson: when you run away from something, you inevitably and simultaneously run toward something. And since Emm had covered her eyes with her hands, she could not see the bank of lockers as she clanged into them.

Clang.

Emm didn't fall. Oh no. Her legs kept churning just enough to keep her upright, spinning around so that she came to a rest with her back against the lockers.

It's all over now, she thought. *They all know me. I couldn't hide it for more than two minutes. Can't do anything right.* Emm pressed her back against the lockers and tried to slide down to the floor, the melodramatic cherry on the sundae of pathetic self-defeat.

But Emm's shirt got caught on a locker hook, suspending her like a morbid puppet. Her slimy hand moved up to rub her bruised forehead, which left her eyes uncovered. Through a veil of tears, and a little mucous, she saw Olly's figure walk through the classroom door toward her.

"Let me help you there," Olly said, gently freeing her from the locker.

"Can't even do a melodramatic slump-down right," Emm said. "I'm a freak and you all know it."

"Listen," Olly started, "not everyone is like that. I'm -" but then Mr. Blake's voice boomed from down the hall.

"Miss Dillinger! You're in distress!" Emm wiped her eyes with her sleeve, trying to clean herself up.

"She's fine, Mr. Blake. I was just helping -"

"Ludicrous," Mr. Blake said to Olly. "She needs guidance and counsel from a grown man. And I am all three of these things. Guidance. Counselor. Grown man." Mr. Blake offered Emm his hand and she took it. She got about a foot off the floor before her lubricated hand gave way and she flomped onto her butt. Olly grabbed her by the waist to pull her up, but Emm needed to use Mr. Blake's head for leverage before finally getting to her feet.

"Sorry," she feebly offered.

"It's going as badly as you feared," Mr. Blake said.

"Worse. All I wanted was a chance to be average, you know? To be a regular kid with a regular life. I'd do anything to have that for just one day."

Olly looked down at his feet.

Mr. Blake thought for a moment, then nodded to himself, grimly. "I have the solution," he pronounced. "My office at once. Not you, Mr. Ford. You can go back to class."

With that, he immediately began marching to his office, expecting Emm to follow. It took her a moment, but she figured it out and sprinted to catch up. She turned to Olly with a smile forming on her lips.

"Thank you," she whispered to him.

Olly waved to her as his smile met hers. Olly felt something warm in his heart and he was reminded of How The Grinch Stole Christmas: Olly's heart felt like it was growing, maybe even three sizes bigger, as he watched the new girl scurry away.

10

Emm sniffed a bit as she sat in a chair across the desk from Mr. Blake. The tempest of shame and self-hatred was starting to subside now that she was back in Mr. Blake's office. He seemed to have a calming effect on Emm and she didn't know why. Maybe because he was a little person. Or an adult. Emm had been around freaks so much that it occurred to her, in this moment, that normal people were the scary ones to her: especially normal people her own age.

Mr. Blake handed her a tissue. "You're going to be fine," he said, then went back to rifling through his drawer, hidden behind his mountains of paperwork.

"Fine? Hinkley's going to flunk me on my first assignment and I managed to hide the fact that I'm a sideshow freak for a grand total of, like, two minutes." Letting that out didn't help make the tears go away. She balled up her tissue.

Mr. Blake's head rose from behind the desk. "Like I said before, Emm, you must rise above." He handed her another tissue.

"I just want to be normal, you know? Why can't anything be normal for me? <bllummppphh>"

Another tissue.

"First of all, what is normal?" It was almost as though Mr. Blake was stalling for time as he searched through his desk. "Who decides what normal is? The majority? What if the majority is wrong? Sane person in an insane world and all that... secondly, why be normal when you can be amazing?" Mr. Blake said. He scrabbled through the drawers of his desk more desperately than before, like he was frustrated. Emm began to forget about her sadness as she got curious about what the heck Mr. Blake was doing.

"Has anyone ever told you how much you look like Snow White?" Mr. Blake said as he fumbled.

"No. What are you doing?"

"You do. Look like Snow White. Now there's a local entrepreneur who knows just what to do with your... natural looks. Mavis Stiles. Ever heard of her?"

"We just moved here, so that would be a no."

"Right. Mavis owns the hottest fashion store in the mall. Spindle. Still nothing?"

Emm shook her head. "I hate the mall."

"Not the majority attitude in this school. Ah. Here it is."

Rising from behind the desk, Mr. Blake lofted his hand high above his head, and dangling from his thick but short fingers was an ancient key on a string of golden fleece. It was the kind of key you'd use to open a massive treasure chest, or the diary of a giant, or prison doors from the dark ages.

"This," he pronounced, "is a key to The Alcove. The VIP area of Spindle. Ask for Mavis and present her with this key."

Are you kidding? "So I should buy new clothes is what you're saying." *Some guidance.*

"No. Fashions. From Spindle." He jiggled the key a bit, but

Emm didn't take the bait.

"Doesn't a guidance counselor say something like 'it's what in you that counts' or 'just be yourself'?"

Mr. Blake scoffed. "This isn't the fifties, Emm. You want to rise above the crowd? Be the belle of the ball. The prettiest princess. The most celebrated celebrity. The – dopest debutante."

"I can't afford it," she said coldly.

Mr. Blake sounded like he was starting to lose his patience. Or perhaps his arm was getting tired from holding the key up and jiggling it for such a long period of time.

"The price will be surprisingly affordable," he said.

"Buying things won't change me," she said.

"It will change what everyone thinks of you," he said.

"Isn't peer pressure supposed to be bad?" Emm did her best Mr. Blake impression, which was really more like an Oscar The Grouch impression. "'Don't worry about what everyone thinks, Emm. You are a strong young woman and they are all just jealous, Emm. Emm, just be yourself.'"

Blake jiggled the key one last time.

"You get these things from Mavis," Blake said, slowly and powerfully, "and they will be jealous all right. Now take the key."

What have I got to lose?

Emm swiped the key out of Mr. Blake's hand.

11

Emm nearly smacked into Olly as she left Mr. Blake's office. He must have been waiting outside for her, but he offered an "oh hey" like he just happened to be there when she just happened to walk out.

"Hey," Emm said, trying to muster up some kindness. "Thanks for helping me."

"Feeling better about life? Being a little different isn't the worst thing in the world, is it?"

"I guess… Mr. Blake gave me some VIP pass to a store? Spindle?" She pulled the key out of her pocket and Olly caressed it. His jaw dropped a little.

"Wow," Olly said. "Only celebutards and runway models get those."

Emm looked at the key a bit harder on this news – and then watched the key get swiped way by the meaty mitt of Letterman Jacket. The big jock casually walked away with her VIP key dangling from his finger.

"John, you ass!" Olly said. Letterman Jacket – John – handed the key to Jessica, who seemed to be surrounded by preppie girl sycophants, and Jessica exalted, like Mary Tyler Moore when she threw her hat in the air: "What?!? I have a key to The Alcove at Spindle?!? Finally!" As though she hadn't ordered John to steal it from Emm in the first place.

All the debutante wannabes around Jessica gathered a little closer and looked at Jessica with even more wonderment, much like the Apostles would have gathered around Jesus, or hyenas around a gazelle carcass, or twitter followers around the famous-for-being-famous.

Grrrr was about all Emm could think. **Grrrr.** One thing Emm had learned over the years, as the scars became calluses: Emm learned how to fight back.

"That's mine!" Emm yelled.

"As if they'd give one of these to a sideshow freak," Jessica said, more to her apostles than to Emm. Giggles cascaded out of the apostles, seemed to pick up steam with the lesser followers who didn't dress quite as well as Jessica, and finally out to the student body at large, which seemed to have congregated like one big landmass around Jessica and John and the key to The Alcove. The entire landmass was quaking with laughter now.

"Excuse me," Olly said as he nudged Emm aside, sidled into the landmass, and tapped John on his beefy elbow, which was as high up as Olly could tap. Olly wasn't sure, but he thought he heard John murmur "come on, give it back" to Jessica.

John turned when Olly tapped his elbow and seemed to grow before Olly's eyes. John probably held a hundred-pound advantage on Olly, and a full foot of height as well. Physically, it was the difference between a man and a Smurf, if there was such a Smurf as Fanboy Smurf. Actually, other Smurfs might have called Olly Shrimpy Smurf. John and Jessica called Olly "Sperm," for reasons that weren't entirely clear to Emm.

"On your bike, Sperm," John dismissed. Olly wouldn't let John's elbow walk away, so John leaned in close. His voice got softer; maybe even gentler. "Don't confront me in front of all these people," he warned Olly.

"What you did was wrong." Olly wouldn't back down.

John used his angry meathead voice again. "Listen, Sperm. If you push me, people will need glasses to see your face in 3D."

Olly wouldn't back down. It made John frustrated.

"Because I will flatten you. Do you not get it? 3D glasses. Flatten your face."

But Olly still wouldn't back down. Instead, he shoved John as hard as he could and nearly succeeded in moving John backwards.

"I tried to warn you," John said, without anger or frustration. He looked fatigued as he put up his dukes and engaged in a pugilist's dance with Olly. Olly raised his fists as well. Jessica backed away, still holding the key high up for all the girls to see. She disappeared into the crowd as the throng pushed forward around Olly and John, ready to watch a fight in the school hallway.

Emm looked at how badly Olly was dwarfed by John. A part of Emm knew that Olly was doing this for the sake of chivalry; to be Emm's knight in whatever whatever. It made Emm feel happy and awful at the same time.

"Stop it!" Emm yelled, reaching for Olly's arms to drag him away. She had two inches and probably twenty pounds on Olly – it wouldn't be a problem to carry him out of there. But two of Jessica's girlfriends grabbed Emm by the arms, holding her in place.

Jessica leaned in from behind, over Emm's shoulder. "Ah-ah-ah, sideshow freak," she whispered to Emm. "Let them fight fair." Jessica's breath on Emm's neck sent a shiver down Emm's spine.

The student body was enthralled with the fight. It was a going to be a crowd-pleaser: Mr. Popular with his letterman jacket, perfect girlfriend, and biceps you could see in a mirror, versus Mr. Irrelevant with his coke bottle glasses, no respect, who people whispered might someday be the kid who traipsed into school wearing the black trenchcoat. Superman versus The Thing Jacob Williams High School Didn't Understand.

"Olly, don't," Emm pleaded, though she could do nothing about it.

Olly stopped, relaxed his arms, and turned to Emm. John relaxed too, as though it were a time out.

"Don't you see, Emm?" Olly began, "We're all just gonna let these mindless idiots do what they please. Just because they're bigger than us, or prettier than us, or on the football team. Well no more! It's time for us weirdoes to take a stand! I'm fighting for all of us!"

No trumpets played a fanfare. No applause smattered. Not a single clap was attempted. No one dared. Not even Lily Farquhar, with the beaded braids and patchouli cloud, who surreptitiously watched the crowd as she read Frankenstein in the lotus position down the hall. Olly didn't speak for her, Lily thought, because Lily had removed herself from the paradigm. *Bunch of meat-eaters,* Lily snickered to herself.

Olly and Emm looked at each other and immediately understood that "all of us" was a group comprised of Oliver Ford and Emily Dillinger and that was it. Olly turned to the crowd and sneered. Then he placed his eyes on John's, way up there, and Olly prepared to fight.

"Last chance," John said.

"What you're doing is wrong. Fight the power!" Olly yelled. "Fight the power! Fight the power!" He tried to start a chant to get himself going. It didn't work.

"Mess with the power," John said, "and the lights go out." In between "power" and "lights go out," John took one easy, beefy swing and nearly decapitated Olly. Olly didn't just fall to the floor unconscious. He flew head-first, spinning like a star-shaped firework, and smacked his shoulder into the floor. Animated things circled Olly's head, and those animated things had animated things circling their heads.

The crowd was completely silent for a moment. The victory was so absolute and instant, they didn't even have a chance for an 'ooh,' although there may have been a 'meh.' They dispersed, somewhat disappointed, and a few kids clapped sarcastically. Emm clasped her mouth in horror. The other debutantes let her go and she ran to Olly.

John stopped her as she tried to kneel at Olly's side.

"I didn't want to hit him," he said. "Tell your boyfriend that. I warned him."

"You suck," is all Emm could say. John's face soured, like her insult had actually hurt his feelings.

"I just know whose side I'm on," he replied. It almost sounded like an apology, which made Emm squint at John curiously. Then, in a flash, Jessica had taken John by the hand and ordered, "Let's go, you're driving me to the mall," and they were gone.

Just like that, Emm was alone with Olly in the hallway. Olly rubbed the side of his head as he came to.

"What do you think? Was I brave or stupid?"

"I guess it was stupid if you're bleeding," Emm said.

Olly checked his fingers, then showed Emm. "No blood. See?"

"Is there a bump?" She tousled his hair, felt around his scalp and found a little one. Emm remembered what her dad used to do when she bonked her head as a kid.

"I kiss better," Emm said with an almost-cutesy voice, and gave the bump on Olly's noggin a gentle, tiny kiss. The kiss worked. Olly woke right up as her lips met his brain. Shocked by the contact, and also the lightning storm of adrenalin bursting through his heart, Olly looked up at Emm and thought long and hard about planting a real kiss on her, a kiss that a boy gives a girl, which would have been Olly's first boy-girl kiss. He felt much better. Better than better.

Emm saw him looking up at her with an unmistakable look on his face. And for a moment, she may have returned the look before she caught herself.

"Wanna meet the Devastating Dillingers of Doom?"

12

Spindle was on the second floor of the Modesta Shopping Center, just past the escalators. The Spindle sign lit up with an almost magical golden glow. The logo of a spindle – an old-timey spinning wheel, like the one they used to spin straw into gold – didn't just glow, it spun with each golden flash, like animated neon lights you'd see in a red light district, or Las Vegas in the sixties.

The window display had all kinds of goodies to draw fashionable customers inside: glass slippers, sequined handbags with "wishes come true" painted on them in graffiti style, a golden ball, aerosol cans of hairspray, pink taffeta prom dresses, picnic baskets, lipsticks, boxes of gingerbread mix, peacock feather earrings, a golden mannequin with sparkling eye shadow, a smartphone cover that said "princess" on it. A quiver full of magic wands.

It was the after school rush. Girls lined up four-wide to get in. Dance music leaked out into the corridor. A security guard, a big African-American guy dressed like The Nutcracker, spoke into his headset and let two more girls inside. The girls were giddy as they walked in. The dance music thrummed with so much bass, the song itself evaded girls' frontal lobes and attacked the medulla oblongata directly, urging their primal amphibian mini-brains to buy, buy, buy and make their fairy tale dreams come true, true, true, by picking up a clutch of straw from a glass display case, or ruby slippers from a shoe shelf, or one of a million other beauty-enhancing products with a fairy tale twist.

At the back of Spindle, two ancient cash registers rang up customers, operated by two odd-looking employees: a rail-thin man who looked to be about two hundred years old; and an overly-pruny old woman with a banana-shaped nose. Past them, behind the cash registers and off to the left a little, a red velvet rope kept one girl from getting to a red velvet curtain.

Behind the red velvet curtain, unseen to those without the exclusive privilege of a key, there was a narrow room that looked more like it belonged in the bottom of a castle than in a mall. Grey stones coated in centuries-old mildew and moss. Long candles in rows lit the room. And at the end of the rows of candles, at the very, very back, just past the very back, there was a woman, who sat at a small café table, sipping some tea and looking at the weathered wooden door just a couple of feet from her.

The woman wore black Louboutins with the trademark red soles and impossibly high spikes. A skin-tight little black number hugged her curves. A black fascinator. Perfect black hair. Perfect tanned skin. Mavis Stiles might have been 50, but she was the hottest female in the mall. Mavis sipped her tea in the back of The Alcove and looked over at the change room door.

"How does it look," she said to the door.

"Ew, there's like, a barrel full of frogs in here. Oh my god," Jessica said on the other side of the door.

Mavis rolled her eyes and tried to sound the part of a

fashion store owner. "Don't mind them. Just try it on and let's have a look at you."

"Mmm. Okay... gurk"

With a creak, the change room door opened. Mavis peeked inside and a murderous grin creeped along her thin lips.

"Why, aren't you a sight," Mavis said. "You look just like... Cinderella! Yes. It's fitting that the first one be a Cinderella. Don't you think?"

Jessica couldn't reply. She was too busy drooling. Jessica's eyes were more vacant than before. She wore a prom dress, not unlike the ones in the front window of Spindle, but the tiara Jessica wore was unlike anything you could buy in the store. It was for VIPs only. There was no shimmer to this tiara. It may have had jewels on it, but the tarnish, rust, patina, decay – whatever you wanted to call it – it was the most rotten-looking piece of jewellery ever placed on a princess's head.

Through the slobber, Jessica tried to form her lips into words. It sounded horrid.

"Am... I... pretty...?" she spewed.

"My dear," Mavis said, eyes glowing, "your wish has come true!"

"You are a princess," Mavis declared as she wiped the drool from Jessica's chin. Jessica twitched a little – perhaps a spasm of joy for having become Cinderella as she had always dreamed. It was difficult to tell.

"Now," Mavis told her, "you get back into that change room, reach into the barrel and get yourself a prince."

13

Olly sat back in the lawnchair and reflected on his day. Any day that involved zombies, fighting, pretty girls and a sideshow freak? Pretty good day. Or maybe that was the concussion talking. He looked out at the spinning circle across the back yard from where he sat; watched it come in and out of focus as his vision went blurry and clear, blurry and clear. It was kind of neat. Almost as neat as the fact that the girl who kissed him was a carny who could throw hatchets at a spinning human being. Then he thought about the kiss on his head and his vision went really blurry.

Emm slid the patio door open and carried a tray through with two ice-cold lemonades on it. Olly conjured up some small talk.

"So you never hit anyone? Even by accident?"

"Nope." Emm plunked the tray down and passed Olly a glass of lemonade. "I did give my stepmom a haircut like Cyndi Lauper once, but I was maybe ten years old, so..." Emm's eyes darted inside. "I thought she would be here." *She's not gonna believe me when I tell her I made a friend.*

"Don't worry about it," Olly said as he held the cold

glass to his temple. "I believe you when you tell me you're a hatchet-throwing Devastating Dillinger."

"Of Doom."

"Of Doom. Otherwise why would you have that thing in your back yard and why would there be a thousand hatchet marks in it?"

"Good point."

They looked everywhere but at each other. The silence seemed to envelop them. The pause was pregnant and it seemed like any moment the little noise baby would pop out and yell "kiss her already!"

At least that's what Olly was thinking.

What to do what to do what to do what to do what to do was actually what Emm was thinking. While she popped the ice cubes into the glasses just a moment earlier, she was thinking about how proud Steph would be that Emm had made the one friend she thought she could never make at school. Now that it was obvious Steph wasn't going to turn up, she wondered what to do and the wonder was going from uncomfortable to panicked.

They both made a move at the same time. Emm's move was to gulp down her lemonade, every last icy sour drop, even if it gave her brain freeze. It was the only trick left in her repertoire. *Maybe I should show him how I can belch,* she thought as she finished the lemonade.

"You're like, the weirdest girl ever," he said, knowing how wrong it sounded the moment it hobbled out of his mouth. That was Olly's move: to call the girl he liked weird.

It stopped Emm from belching. Instead, Emm could do nothing but smile and try to mask the sting. *Thanks.*

Olly tried again. "Like as if Snow White shopped at vintage

stores..." he immediately realized Emm wasn't looking pleased and blurted "weird is good, you know. I'm weird."

As the hatchet wheel turned lazily, a small drop of sweat trickled down Olly's forehead and into his eye. He grimaced a little, but the grimace was really from replaying his own stupidheaded words in his dumb brain.

"Does it still hurt?" Emm offered like a bridgeside life preserver.

Olly talked in slooow motion. "Con-con-shun ... brain dam-age ... no, it's fine. Little headache. So you wanna do something? Wanna see that Spindle place?"

Olly moved a little closer. Emm moved a little back.

"I hate the mall," she said.

"Me too."

"Let's do it. But with irony," she said.

"Yeah, like the hipsters do. Meta, bro."

Emm got them the hell out of there before the moment could feel any more uncomfortable for her.

14

The lineup outside Spindle was ridiculous. It was like Justin Beiber was about to play in there, or a cooler version of Justin Beiber. There must have been two hundred girls standing four-wide, silently and grumpily, behind the barricade fence that ran along the corridor. There was no way Emm was going to wait in line.

Emm walked up to the security guard with a strut that said she didn't just belong in line, she belonged at the head of it. Olly did the same, but really played it up, limping and dragging his back foot like a ol' skool pimp. Emm looked back at him and nearly burst out laughing. The security guard didn't even smirk.

"My good man," Emm said in her best British upper-crusty accent, "I am due to get my super-duper-beauty treatment from Mavis and she told me to get my key in there. The key to the back roomie thing."

"The Alcove."

"Righty right right, my good man," she said, trying not to overdo the British accent and failing. The security guard didn't even look at them. He surveyed the girls, making sure no one attempted so much as a cut in line.

Olly chimed in and his accent was some kind of hybrid

of Australian, Kiwi and South African. "Let us through, sport," he said, "or I'll ja-ha-ha your krellins, I will. Count it up and throw it down. Got me?"

The security guard and Emm both looked at Olly like he had eaten a bird.

"Back of the line, nerd kids."

"I do declare!" Emm said.

The security guard puffed up his chest, which was about as big around as Olly if Olly had curled up on the floor.

"You got it mixed up," the guard told Emm. "That's Southern Belle, not British aristocrat. If you're gonna mock me than at least have the good sense to – hold on." The security guard tapped his earpiece. A voice crackled through the guard's headset into his ear, and whatever the voice said, it made the security guard scowl.

"Welcome to Spindle, your majesties," the guard said flatly, and let them cut through the line, to a rousing chorus of boos and hisses.

The banana-nosed old lady greeted them at the cash counter.

"Welcome to Spindle. May I help?" Banana-Nose croaked. The voice sounded like the dryest, oldest old lady voice Emm had ever heard.

Emm got into character. "Oh like hi," she bubbled, "I like lost my key to The Alcove thing? But I should so be in there. Can't you see? I mean, look at my perfect teeth."

Olly examined her teeth like a dentist would. "Yes," Olly said, moving Emm's chin to show Banana-Nose the teeth. "Don't you see? These teeth are perfect!"

Banana-Nose looked at them like she knew they were

goofing around, and it was not even the slightest bit funny. "You're not ready for The Alcove, deary," she said, and went back to book-keeping with her pencil and ledger.

"Excuse me," Olly said, "should she be taking that personally?" He turned to Emm. "I think you should be taking that personally."

"No, no, no," Banana-Nose said. "You need some accessories. To be ready. Some accessories." She tore the page out of her ledger and handed it to Emm. It was a list:

1) Wear the Oro Fleece Poncho,

2) Drink from the Crystahll Couture Water Vessel,

3) Apply the Skin Deep Beauty Ointment.

"What is this?" Emm said.

"First things first and one at a time, yes? First things first and one at a time." Banana-Nose started to twiddle her fingers. "Oro Fleece... Oro Fleece... what is the date?"

"May sixteenth?" Olly said as he wondered exactly why that was important. *Two days* til prom was another thought that crept in there.

Banana-Nose pulled a chart out from a drawer. It was a big, calendar-looking sheet with moon and sun phases on it. Emm and Olly looked at each other like their brains were texting "WTF" to each other. Using a facial expression was a commonly-used means of transmitting feelings like WTF in situations such as this.

"Yes..." Banana-Nose went on, pointing a gnarled finger at the junction of two axes on her chart. "Yes, precisely at 8:11. 8:11 tonight, look to the sun and raise a clutch of straw in your hand for one minute. At 8:12, you will be holding your fleece. Hold up the straw at 8:11 as you look to the sun."

Emm could only manage a stunned "what?"

Olly said, "wait a minute, wait a minute. So this fleece is not for sale in the store?"

"Oh, I am losing my mind in my old age," Banana-Nose said with a facepalm, "Clutches of straw... yes, just beneath the glass slippers on that shelf."

"Wait another minute," Olly said. "You're saying that you sell straw in this girly fashion store? And if we buy some of the straw that you're actually trying to sell in this store, and hold it up into the sky, it will magically turn into... a poncho?"

"No. The straw is not for sale. It's free. And it's right over there."

Emm and Olly looked at each other. Then looked to where Banana-Nose was pointing. Then looked back at each other and shrugged. They left for the straw shelf, just beneath the glass slippers.

As soon as they left, Banana-Nose picked up the phone and covered her mouth as she spoke.

"She's not ready yet," she crackled into the phone. "She lost the key... lost it!"

At the display case that displayed the bizarre pairing of glass slippers and allegedly-magical straw, Emm and Olly stood spellbound. There was indeed a miniature hay bale of straw, and a little card that said "FREE" in front of it.

"Do you believe this?" Olly said, really just for something to say.

"No, I don't believe it. Magic isn't real. It's some kind of illusion," Emm said.

"So... you gonna try it?"

"Of course not!"

Olly put on his best bulbous-eyed freakazoid magician impression, complete with waving hands painting magical rainbows in the air: "I thought you believed in the magic of the sun, with all our wishes on the nearest star coming true..." he smiled proudly at his own joke.

Emm tried to mask the sting again with a poor excuse for a smile. *He's making fun of me. He thinks my ideas are a joke. He thinks I'm a joke, just like everyone else.*

"A fleece would keep you warm during the great global ice age you mentioned in your speech..."

"I should probably get home," Emm said, and made for the exit.

"Wait –"

"See you at school." She marched away.

Olly grabbed a handful of straw, stuffed it into his shirt, and chased after Emm. He caught up to her as she left the store. She didn't stop walking. Steam was beginning to condense into tears.

How could I think this guy was any different? She thought.

"If I said something wrong, I'm sorry..." he offered.

"No problem," Emm said curtly, not breaking her stride.

"When I'm nervous I poke fun, okay? It's what I do. Can't help it."

"Why are you nervous? You're not the one getting mocked." She wouldn't slow down.

They marched so quickly, Olly began to feel winded. He knew he couldn't keep this pace up. She was losing him. Olly had one last chance to ask Emm the question he'd been wanting to ask since he clapped eyes on Emm this morning. He took a big gasp of air and went for it, the words shooting out of him like a machine gun: "Cause there's this school prom coming up and all day I've been thinking to myself 'ask her, ask her,' and I've never felt like that before and I've never done anything like that before, which makes me very nervous but screw it here goes… Emm, will you go to prom with me?"

That made Emm stop. It made her stop and think about the kiss.

"I've known you for one day," she said.

"Try it. Risk-free. Cancel at any time."

Emm had led him on and she realized it in this very moment. The kiss on the head, meant to be kind and caring, had backfired big-time. Now Olly was crushing on her and thinking romance, and all Emm could think of was an entire school who laughed at them. The last thing she wanted to do was make a display of herself at prom. "I can't, Olly."

Olly grabbed his chest. *Is this his idea of a joke?* Emm thought.

"I don't want a date. I want a friend," she said. With that, Olly fell to his knees, still clutching his chest (where the straw was stuffed), and grunted. "I think I'm having – a heart attack."

Emm's eyes widened with fear and rage. "Help…" Olly said, but all Emm could see was

The Amazing Derek Dillinger
falling from his wheelchair
into the desert sand

clutching his chest.

How could Olly know? How could he do this to me?

She ran from there as fast as she could. Barrelled through a couple of seniors as she hit the escalator and ran down each stair. *Never going to the mall again,* she cried to herself.

"Emm…" Olly groaned, "Emm, it really hurts." Olly thought he was going to die. When she said "friend," it felt like someone was squeezing his heart in the palm of their hand. But as Emm left the mall, whatever was squeezing Olly's heart seemed to let go just a little, and he was able to limp out of the mall in agony, and agony was better than he had felt when Emm was breaking his heart.

15

Emm rushed through the house, slammed her bedroom door and flopped onto her bed. She didn't even call out to see if Steph was home and she didn't wait to hear if Steph would yell hello from wherever she was. Emm was running too fast. Running for her pillow, the only place that was safe.

She buried her head in that pillow and nearly chewed on it. *It's a disaster*, she thought. *I can't do this anymore*, she thought. The thoughts became a fever that burned in the pit of her stomach. She let a blubber fall into her pillow and the blubber grew into a wail. Emm felt like she just wasn't equipped for real life – normal life. Once a freak show, always a freak show.

Never forget who we are, her dad had said in his final breath.

Thanks a lot, Dad. We're the butt of everyone's joke. Even Olly's. We're the loser weirdoes. That's who we are.

Emm let it all out, but it never seemed to reach the end. She buried her head even deeper into the pillow and screamed at the top of her lungs. Screamed all of the anger and loneliness and pain out.

I'm all alone. And where are you, Dad? Where are you?

Meanwhile, the clock radio beside her bed went from 8:10 to 8:11

16

In his back yard, Olly used every ounce of his might to lift the clutch of straw up to the sky. He looked into the sun and squint-grimaced. While one hand held up the straw, the other clutched his chest, which still hurt like a mofo. Olly couldn't clench his jaw any tighter. He trembled in the throes of his never-ending heart attack.

Then it became too much.

He pulled at his shirt and looked down. The shirt stretched so much, his collar pulled down over his nipple and Olly could see something bubbling beneath the flesh, right above his heart. He cried out so loud that it echoed in the valley of McMansion back yards.

A piece of iron broke through Olly's skin and rose like a charmed snake from his chest.

Then a second iron snake came out.

Then a third.

They weaved into one another like a braid, then another braid, then spread out and buried themselves back into Olly's chest.

Olly panted in terror. He could feel the metal snakes moving - *weaving* - inside his chest cavity, swimming around in his muscles and blood. It hurt like nothing Olly had ever felt.

The iron snakes swam for the surface again.

They pierced his flesh in a new place and Olly bellowed in agony once again. The three iron snakes weaved two more braids, buried themselves into his chest a final time, and left Olly's heart inside a metal cage.

They sealed themselves up with a jailhouse clang.

The torture was over. He knocked on the metal as if to see whether he was dreaming it. He wasn't.

When Olly pulled his other hand down to give the new metal bars around his heart a two-handed tug, he absently tossed the Oro Fleece Poncho to the grass. He didn't even realize the straw had been transformed while he tugged at the heart-cage in a panic. In his terror, Olly didn't realize the pain had disappeared, either. His heart was safe and sound in its new home.

Olly's mom came out of the back door, staggered up to him as he wrestled with himself, and cuffed him on the back of the head. "You're grounded, idiot," she said. "Get inside. You're an embarrassment!" He came to his senses when she cuffed the back of his head a second time. Then he got up, scooped up the Oro Fleece Poncho, and sulked into the house as his mother called him a priss for owning a gold shawl.

17

When Emm woke up in the morning, Steph was already making eggs. Steph looked over at Emm with her extreme bed head and black pajamas and it reminded Steph of when Emm was little. She was always a grumpy mess in the mornings, and that was one thing that hasn't changed, Steph thought.

"Where were you," Emm mewed as she sat at the breakfast nook.

"Working. I got mega-overtime last night." Steph perked up a little and asked, "so, how was the first day?! You make a friend? Meet a cute boy?"

"I'm dropping out."

"You're what? No you're not. Eat this." Steph plunked some eggs down on the table and sat down to watch Emm eat them.

"I'm sixteen, Steph. I have the legal right to drop out. I googled it. I can just write my GED and bam, I'm employable."

Steph didn't seem too impressed. "Employable as what? Taco stuffer? Latté foamer?"

"Maybe I can just be a carny."

"If there's one thing you can't do, you and I both know it's that."

"I can be a mailman. Or go to college on the internet."

"Wildlife forestry management. Great choice." Steph slid the plate of eggs away from Emm midway through a scoop and got up. "You're gonna quit after one day. I thought you were tough. I thought you were going to try and make one friend yesterday. That was the goal."

"I made a friend. At least I thought he was a friend, but he turned out to be... not a friend. Got in a scrap."

"You what?"

"Nothing. Some kid got in a fight. Not me."

"Oh... so the speech went all right?"

"No."

"The other kids were okay?"

"Nope."

"What about that guidance counselor, Mr. um..."

"Blake. Nope. Crazy little person whose advice for me was to go shopping. The mall, by the way? Sucks."

"It does suck, and you can expect to work there for the rest of your life if you don't finish high school."

"I'm not going back, Steph."

Steph smashed the plate into the sink in frustration, then reeled it back in. "You can't quit, Emm. Just... forget yesterday ever happened, okay? Whatever comes at you today, at school, just roll with it. All right? Maybe the friend who you thought was a friend but wasn't a friend is actually a friend after all. Sometimes school can be dramatic like that."

Emm tried to rub the sleep out of her eyes.

"You ever been in that Spindle store? It's the weirdest place ever. Trying to make girls into fairy tale princesses.

Who would want that?"

"Hmm... like every teenaged girl in a hundred-mile radius?"

"That explains why I hate them all so much."

"Be open-minded, sweetie. Okay? For me. One more day. Go back to Mr. Blake and switch classes, or get him to help you. That's what he's there for. Guidance. And maybe if he gives you some advice you think is bogus, just roll with it and see where it gets you. Okay? Who knows, maybe his advice will be different today."

Emm nodded, which made Steph smile.

18

Dressed head-to-toe in her very darkest black outfit, the only non-black item being the white logos of her Chuck high-tops Black Flag t-shirt, Emm kept her headphones over her ears so no one would try to talk to her. She hid her discman in her black backpack so no one could see it. Emm's music thing looked huge and dumb compared to everybody else's little iPod thingies. Emm played her L7 disc, *Bricks are Heavy*. She loved the song "Pretend We're Dead" and she played it over and over.

Armed with the angry Grrrl music and her black suit of armor, Emm was starting to feel okay. Maybe even invulnerable. Mr. Blake's office was dead ahead, and she was going to tell him exactly what she wanted to do – transfer classes, no Jessica and John and especially no Olly – and if he didn't do it, she was the eff out of there. He didn't want to doom her to a life of retail McSlavery, did he?

From out of nowhere, Olly swooped in between her and the door. Olly held a golden fleece poncho in his hand.

"Sun magic works," he said, and Emm nearly took the

bait, forgetting for a moment that she now hated Olly.

"Sperm. Olly," a voice boomed from behind Emm. It was John. Olly whipped the poncho behind his back as John approached with haste, his feet making the floor rumble with each step. Emm got in John's way.

"Leave him alone, John. You're a big tough ape, we get it."

"No," John said. His face registered panic. "I need your help. Something is wrong with Jessica."

"What," Emm said, "was she nice to someone? Did she pet a small furry animal? What could possibly be wrong with Miss Perfect?"

"I think – I think she might be a zombie." John whispered the 'zombie' part.

"You're dumber than you look," Olly said.

"Come with me. Please. I'll give you anything if you come and see."

"Anything?" Olly said with a mischievous grin. "Okay. Okay. If I go, you have to be my personal bodyguard, servant, slave, vassal, fight my battles for me, do anything I ask."

"Deal," John said with no hesitation. "Let's go."

"Where are we going?" Emm said.

"Class. She sat down early."

"Oh my god," Olly said. "Something is definitely wrong."

As they headed for class, Olly handed Emm the poncho. Emm slid it on.

"Perfect fit," Olly said with an uneasy smile.

Open mind, open mind. "We need to talk," Emm said, "Later."

19

Emm peeked into the classroom from the doorway. There was Jessica, sitting at her desk with perfect posture. There was a tarnished tiara on her Barbie-blonde hair. The vacant stare of normal Jessica seemed amplified.

(Unbeknownst to anyone, a slimy little frog poked its slimy little eyes out from between the buttons of Jessica's designer cardigan and had a look around. It didn't see any flies and didn't see any lilypads and didn't see any damsels in distress, so it popped its head back inside Jessica's shirt. Unbeknownst to anyone.)

Olly came around Emm and took a look for himself. He pointed at the tiara. "See? She really does think she's a princess," Olly whispered.

John didn't bother with any stealth or sneakiness. He just clomped right up to Jessica and barked "Jess. Jessica." He leaned over her, his hands on her desk, and brought his face right up to hers. She didn't respond.

Emm and Olly came up behind John. Jessica's face twitched a little and her mascara ran. Drool ran from the corner of her mouth. There was definitely something zombie-like about her. John waved a hand in front of her eyes to see if she was blind.

"See?" John said. "Nothing going on in there."

"That doesn't prove anything," Olly said. "I don't see any necrotizing, though. What else... well, she's not eating brains, either, so I tend to believe, therefore, that she is not a –"

Suddenly, Jessica's eyes darted to Emm's chest. It made all three of them gasp in unison. Jessica's lips quivered and began to move. "She's trying to say something," John said.

A long, belabored "ohhh" came from Jessica's throat.

John came in closer, his hand tightening on Jessica's shoulder. "Jess?"

"Ohhhhm –" It was Jessica's voice but, at the same time, it wasn't. It was an ugly, monstrous voice that gurgled with bile and brimstone. It was unnatural and barely human.

Jessica's eyes never left Emm's chest. Emm put her hand where she thought Jessica was looking – and remembered that the opal heart-shaped pendant that her dad gave her was hiding underneath the poncho and shirt, which is where it always was, since she never took it off. The whitish jewelled heart rolled beneath Emm's hand a little.

"Talk to me, baby. What's wrong?" John pleaded.

It burst out of Jessica like a volcanic eruption. In a magmatic, monstrous voice, she blurted out, "ohhhhmygod where did you get that?"

Emm picked at the poncho. "Uh, this? Spindle?"

The drooling, twitching debutante corked her head slightly, as though she was trying to remember. "Spindle..."

"I took her there yesterday." John said. "With the key I took from you."

How come she was ready to go into The Alcove but I'm not? "You saw Mavis?"

Jessica didn't really answer. Instead, she pushed John away from her and turned to face Emm with a new wild energy in her bulging, mascara-soaked eyes.

"Cinderella, Cinderella, all I am is Cinderella," the voice inside Jessica growled as she launched herself at Emm, grabbed a handful of the golden fleece, and pulled it halfway off Emm, dragging them both into the desks. The desks groaned as they slid along the floor, loud and awful like a flock of ducks being run over by a semi.

In the hubbub, the slimy little frog escaped from Jessica's top and hopped out of class. Only Lily Farquhar shrieked at the sight of it, which made Lily quite ashamed since she loved nature so much.

Hitting desks hurts, it occurred to Emm, as she struggled to escape the poncho that now held her prisoner, like a straightjacket or a hockey jersey one player pulls it over the other's head. Jessica held Emm in the straightjacket by pulling wildly at the poncho. Emm could hear some students squeal as they walked into class. She could also hear Olly shouting, "protect your brain! Protect your brain!"

Emm bashed into desk after desk, hurting her hip and kneecap as Jessica growled like an animal and pulled even harder. The poncho wasn't coming off and Jessica was tugging Emm around like a big puppet. Emm felt her feet leave the floor as her body stretched over a couple of desks. *I'd really like to see right now. Mostly so I could punch the snot out of this biatch.*

Emm felt a beefy arm slide around her waist and two hands wrap around her ankles. They pulled her back, but Jessica's strength was such that Emm just stretched like a gold and black rubber band for a moment.

Finally, Jessica slipped and Emm flew back into the boys. Emm found her feet and yanked the poncho down, finally being able to see. Jessica was inches from Emm, clawing at Emm's chest. If Jessica was a zombie, she wasn't interested in brains, but hearts might be a possibility.

"Hey, eyes up here!" Emm shouted. But Jessica's eyes didn't move.

"Mine," the monstrous voice inside Jessica snarled. Jessica pounced, but John grabbed her by the waist to keep Emm from another melee. But John wasn't quite quick enough and Jessica got a mouthful of the only thing her teeth could reach: Emm's wrist. Emm cried out in pain and Jessica's smile sunk into her wrist a little further.

Just then, Mr. Hinkley walked into the classroom. He looked up from his papers to see the swath of collided desks and Jessica's mouth latched on to Emm's wrist.

"Not cool, guys," Mr. Hinkley warned. Emm pulled one way and John pulled another to get Emm out of Jessica's mouth, and as John twisted her away, Jessica's saliva flew like a wave and rained down, soaking the desks, John, and a couple of students who cringed against the wall. Drops of spittle even reached Mr. Hinkley's face.

Mr. Hinkley wiped his cheek. "I don't get paid for this," he said to himself, spun on his heel, and walked out.

The bite really hurt. It also made Emm think twice about beating this girl up, even if she deserved it. Who bites like that? Something was definitely wrong with Princess Jessica, and being a zombie seemed to describe it about as well as anything.

"Mine," Jessica said again. She struggled so relentlessly that John was starting to weaken.

"You want it?!" Emm shrieked, pulling the poncho off. "Take

it!" Emm threw it at Jessica.

Jessica stopped struggling. She buried her face in the poncho and rooted around the way pig sniffs for truffles or a dog sniffs a new's dog butt. John carried her back to her seat and plopped her in it. All Jessica did was continue to bury her face in the golden fleece poncho.

Emm inspected her wrist – two tooth-shaped holes filled up with blood. The adrenaline started to subside and Emm's lungs tried to catch up. *She tried to kill me,* Emm thought. *High school is so not worth all of this.*

"Are you all right?" Olly said. His face came so close to Emm's that she backed away.

"She wouldn't have rabies or anything, right? Or be a vampire, right?"

Olly shrugged. They shared a worried look.

"I'm glad you're okay," Olly said. "Hey, whatever I did to make you run away, I'm sorry. The last thing I want you to do is run away."

Feelings talks never made Emm very comfortable. Thankfully, John called her name and tossed the poncho back to her. Jessica's eyes still did not leave the poncho.

"You have the necklacccce," Jessica hissed at Emm. Emm clutched the pendant that hid beneath her shirt and prepared for Jessica to launch herself again – but Mr. Blake walked in at that exact moment. Mr. Hinkley was a couple of steps behind, arms crossed as though he had been wronged.

"Emily Dillinger. Oliver Ford. John Rockwell. Jessica Jones. Office. Now."

John stepped in front of Jessica. "Mr. Blake, Jessica is – sick or something."

"I'm the guidance counselor, not the school nurse. Now move. All of you."

No problem, Emm thought as she took the opportunity to get out of there. The moment Emm left Jessica's field of vision, the vacant stare returned. Mr. Blake glared at John expectantly. John scooped Jessica up by the waist and carried her out like a plank of wood.

"Not cool, guys," Hinkley threw at them as they passed, but he still pressed his back up against the wall when they went by.

20

"I heard there was a fracas yesterday, as well," Mr. Blake said.

John nodded. The four kids sat in a row across Mr. Blake, barely able to fit inside his office. John was the only one who could see Mr. Blake's face through the piles of paperwork.

"Uh, big misunderstanding," Emm said, eager to get out of there. "Won't happen again. Right, guys?"

"Never, Mr. Blake," John said. "I made a promise."

"Oliver?"

"It's true. We've made our peace with it," Olly said, though he didn't entirely mean it.

"Jessica, anything to add?" Mr. Blake stood up and peered around a pile to make eye contact with her. Jessica twitched, eyes transfixed on a power outlet, and then a houseplant, and then Emm's chest. And then the power outlet. There was no stopping the drool escaping the corner of her downturned mouth.

"I find your behavior disconcerting, Jessica. Not to mention your tiara."

"Hey," John nudged Emm. "Pull out that shawl thing."

Show Mr. Blake."

"No way!" Emm said, clutching the backpack where it hid a little tighter.

"Shawl?" Mr. Blake said? "A poncho? From Spindle?"

"Yeah, here. This." Reluctantly, Emm reached for her backpack to pull it out.

Mr. Blake leaped out from behind the desk. "No no no no!" he said in a panic. Then he put on a smile and said, very calmly, "It's all right. While we don't have a dress code at Jacob Williams High School, I think we can all agree that it is preposterous to believe someone would have the audacity to sport a crown, laurels, scepter or tiara in an educational setting. I must insist that Jessica remove the tiara."

Jessica had something to say to this suggestion.

"Kkkkkkkk."

"John," Mr. Blake said, "kindly pass the tiara to me." As soon as he said it, Jessica rose to her feet like a robot and turned for the door.

"Quickly, John," Mr. Blake urged.

John reached for the tiara and Jessica snapped her jaws at him like a yip dog.

"Baby, Mr. Blake said..."

"Kkkkkkkk," Jessica replied venomously. She staggered out of the office. John gave chase.

Emm and Olly looked at each other, then Mr. Blake, then at each other again. *He figured it out,* Emm thought. *Jessica used the key. I'm in so much crap.*

"Go!" Mr. Blake said. "Get the tiara."

Emm slithered out of her chair and pushed Olly to get out of there.

"Emm," Mr. Blake called and Emm froze. *Crap.* Olly was gone, too. "She got the key, didn't she?" *Double crap.* Emm lowered her head to attempt a shamed look. She wasn't feeling that much regret, though, what with Jessica being turned into a zombie instead of Emm. Avoiding zombification tended to prevent feelings of regret.

Mr. Blake went behind his desk, opened his drawer, and pulled out another key – an identical ancient key dangling from a golden string. "Um. No thanks," Emm said. "Have you seen Jessica?"

"Jessica is just... feeling pretty... as she recovers from Mavis's beauty treatment." He pressed the key into Emm's palm. "Don't waste another moment. Let those boys deal with the tiara. Get to Spindle at once."

"I have class."

"You are excused for the day. Off you go."

"But –"

"Go. Now."

And Emm left. As soon as she was gone, Mr. Blake leapt for the phone and pressed one on the speed dial.

"I had to give her a second key," he growled. "No, we don't have time... no... she was *born* ready." Mr. Blake slammed down the phone. And prayed to the moon that it wasn't too late.

21

It's wasn't too difficult for Emm catch up to the others. Jessica was staggering, very zombielike, down the hall – one Jessica wannabe spotted her coming and started her own stagger, Jessica-style – John and Olly walked carefully behind.

Another girl approached Jessica. "Oh my god megahot tiara. I so need one of those. Spindle, right?"

"KkkkkkkkSpindlekkkkkk," Jessica gurgled.

"I know, right?" The girl pulled out a key of her own, but Jessica shuffled past without paying any mind. "Getting one tonight!" The girl called, but didn't get the Jessica approval she had hoped for. Jessica made a slow beeline for the girls' restroom.

"How do we help her?" John asked.

With another "kkkkkkk," Jessica pushed the restroom door open. Her hands stayed at her sides. She pushed the door open with her face.

"Guys," said Emm, blessed with the mutant power of stating the obvious, "something really bad is happening here."

Olly clapped his fist into his palm like he had an action plan. "We should go to Spindle and fut shik up," he said, "before sun magic turns all of us into that."

"Did you seriously just say 'fut shik up'?" Emm said.

"You guys do what you need to do," John said, "I'm not leaving her."

"Ah, but you made a promise. You go where we go," Olly said.

"Even though the world's worst guidance counselor just gave me another VIP key, we're not leaving," Emm said. "Besides, we don't know sun magic did anything bad."

"What do you make of this, then?" Olly said, and pulled his Iron Maiden t-shirt up high enough to display the metal bands that caged his heart through his flesh and bone.

Emm's fingers trembled as they touched the metal. She remembered Olly clutching his chest in the mall. *He wasn't messing with me. He wasn't poking fun. This is real.* Emm looked up into Olly's eyes and tried to make apologetic words come from her lips. All her lips did was tremble.

"I didn't wish for this to happen, Emm. So maybe sun magic works, but not how you think it does."

"I'm so sorry," Emm said.

"Double-u tee eff," John said, but he wasn't looking at Olly. John hadn't averted his eyes from the restroom and Jessica had just emerged, arm in arm with a handsome boy. The boy looked thin and trendy, decked out in American Apparel clothes with a Coldplay-style military jacket, complete with epaulets. The boy's jacket reminded Emm of the security guard's jacket at Spindle. Like a prince and princess, they strode regally away from John. He chased them down.

"Jess," John started, but the handsome boy said "begone" as they continued to make their procession down the hall.

"Who are you?" John said to him.

"The lady is mine. Begone, I say, ox-faced oaf."

John was so crushed he couldn't help but confront Jessica. "You cheat on me two days before prom? With this guy and his douchey hipster talk? This sucks, Jess. I even practiced a dance move for you. You know how much I hate Michael!"

The handsome boy spun, surprising John, and pushed big John into the lockers. Somehow, mid-spin, the boy had managed to pull a dagger out from within his jacket and presently pointed the tip of it into the hollow of John's throat. Jessica stopped and stared into space.

"I'll make ye a gelding afore ye can cry for mercy, ox-face. Now begone!" John raised his hands and backed off.

"Who are you? Who are you?" John said, once to Jessica and once to her new boyfriend. Tears welled up in John's eyes as the boy took Jessica's arm. "Get your hand off of her, Sargeant Pepper!"

"I'm Prince Charming, lugheaded lummox," he told John. Then Prince Charming said "kkkkkk" to Jessica and Jessica said "kkkkkk" back to him and they continued down the hall and out of school.

"What in the hell was that?" Olly said as they caught up.

"Wanna go shopping?" John said, his face now completely red. "Let's go shopping." And he led Emm and Olly to his red convertible.

22

As they reached the top of the escalator and marched toward Spindle, Emm tried to gather her thoughts. In a span not much longer than twenty-four hours, she had confirmed that magic was indeed real, Olly was possibly a friend who had become a victim of said magic, and Olly had now earned himself a permanent slave/man-servant. Plus the girl who ruined any chance of Emm becoming a normal kid for the next two years of high school had been transformed into some kind of zombie, all because she went to the mall with a stolen key that her evil guidance counselor had forced upon Emm. Emm wondered if Steph would be so keen about school if Emm told her what was going on. Plus Mr. Blake's whole giving-her-a-second-key thing likely meant that Emm was being sent into a trap. Not only that, Emm was marching right into it.

"Yeah," Emm said as she stopped. "Maybe we should think this over."

"What's there to think about?" Olly said. "The store has magic stuff in it."

"And somehow, if I use this key, I get turned into – Jessica."

"Right. A zombie with a tiara. Sorry, John."

John looked at his size-fourteens. "Don't forget about Prince Charming."

"A fairy tale store," Emm said. "Why?"

"Jess was crazy about being a princess," John said. "That's just who she was... who she is. Maybe the zombie thing is her wish coming true somehow. I thought I was her Prince Charming, but..."

Olly touched his metal heart cage. "Maybe it's an unintended side effect," he thought out loud. And that reminded Emm of another thing her dad said on the day he died in the desert.

"The universe wills it and it is so..."

"Yeah, maybe the universe wants me to get my butt out of here," Emm said.

"Please, Emm," John said, threatening to kneel, "I can't do this without you."

"Don't worry, John," Olly said with an eye to Emm, "we got your back. Come on, Emm. Let's do this, A-Team style."

Emm had no idea what Olly was talking about, but she took one step toward Spindle, and then another, and another, until she was showing the security guard her key to the Alcove and skipping the lineup – which was longer than ever, despite it being about 9:30 in the morning on a school day.

They marched up to Banana-Nose at the cash register. She looked pleased to see Emm.

"You're back. May I see the Oro Fleece Poncho? May I see?"

Emm pulled it out of her backpack. "Where's Mavis?" she ordered. "We know what's going on around here."

Banana-Nose felt the fabric of the poncho and exalted, "Isn't it wonderful? Wonderful! Oh, you'll see Mavis. Soon as you complete the three tasks and carry with you the three accessories. Three."

"Oh, no no. I have a key," Emm said and dangled it again.

"And I have melanoma," the crone said. "Let's set you on your second task, shall we? Water bottles are right over there."

"Isn't this a key to The Alcove? You said –"

"Tell her about my chest!" Olly hissed.

"Yes, that is a key, but your journey doesn't take you to The Alcove until you've got your things."

"But our friend just got in there yesterday," John said. "She just walked right in."

"She must have been ready," Banana-Nose said. "I don't make the rules. I work the cash register. Crystahll Couture Water Vessels... right over there, deary. Pick one and open it... open it."

With a sigh, Emm led the boys in the direction the old lady's gnarled finger pointed. They arrived at a shelf of water bottles, dozens of them, all made of prismatic crystal that sparkled with rainbow effects, like Faberge eggs or bottles of booze that rappers would pour on the ground or on girls in rap videos.

Emm turned to John.

"I'm doing this to help the girl who made my first day of school a living hell, and you didn't help much either. You see the irony in this, right?"

"You are a saint," John said. "I will always be grateful for your help. Always."

"If I do this, and something happens to me, like I turn green or get transported to Narnia or grow a third boob—"

"—Or grow boobs at all," Olly said. "Sorry."

"If something happens to me..."

"We won't let anything happen to you," John said.

"Right," Olly said, "no matter what."

"Unless everything turns into normalville and I become a totally vanilla, regular, normal girl who never grew up in a traveling circus sideshow. That you can let happen to me."

Emm took a bottle from off the shelf.

"Here goes," she said. The boys gave final words of encouragement.

She twisted the cap off the bottle.

23

Nothing happened.

Emm shook the Crystahll Couture Water Vessel. Nothing in it. She turned it around and checked for a label. Nothing. She tilted the bottle up to the ceiling and peeked into it with one eye.

A rolled-up piece of paper slid out, nailing her in the cornea.

"Ack!"

"Are you okay?" Olly said as she dropped the bottle. John dove and scooped up the fumble with his football reflexes.

"Duh, we won't let anything happen to you, ever ever never," Emm said in her best 'dumb boy' voice. "Ow," she added for punctuation.

John picked up the paper and unrolled it as Emm rubbed her eye.

"Fill me with the water from Old Man Johnson's well at sunset," John read aloud.

"Old Man Johnson?" Emm asked.

"It turns grey and gets all shrivelly," Olly said. No one laughed. "Old man's johnson?" Nothing but glares. "I'm nervous, all right? Jeez."

"Old Man Johnson's well is at Memorial Park," John said.

Olly pointed over to The Alcove and said, "hey, isn't that Lily Farquhar?" They all looked over to see Lily, the granola girl who was better than all of them, sporting a tarnished tiara and staggering away from The Alcove's open doorway. Mavis reached for the red velvet curtain and closed it as Lily drooled her way through the store.

"She got zombified," Emm said. *She was ready for The Alcove too! What is wrong with me?*

"Silly Lily? Are you serious?" Olly said.

Lily seemed to be staggering toward them. "Let's get out of here before she sees your poncho," John said, and they headed for John's car and Old Man Johnson's well.

With vacant eyes and a heart filled with pride, Princess Lily Farquhar and her new Frog Prince made their way home.

24

No one really felt the need to remember whatever was memorialized at Memorial Park, and no one really wanted to be outdoors, plus there was some good tv on, so Memorial Park was empty when John's red convertible rolled up to the park. They hopped out and John led them through a cluster of trees. An old stone well was visible on the horizon, maybe half a mile away. John marched ahead Emm and Olly, with purpose, with a mission in his mind. Emm wasn't in such a rush to do more magical things.

"Why did you hold the straw up to the sun?" she asked Olly.

Olly smiled like the jig was up. "To give you what you wanted," he said. "I mean you wanted the fleece, not the –"

"– The metal things," she said. They were quiet for a moment, not sure what to say about what happened to Olly.

"I think they go all the way around my heart," he said. "I feel them inside me. Like the metal squeezes my heart sometimes. I don't know if my heart is growing or the metal is shrinking..."

"Wait," Emm said as it occurred to her, "there's a fairy tale like that. My dad read it to me... the frog's servant had metal bands around his heart to keep his heart from breaking."

Olly looked away. *I broke his heart,* Emm thought.

"I can't help what I feel, Olly. And neither can you. I do think you're a good friend."

Every boy would rather take a kick to the nards than hear 'friend' uttered in response to a romantic overture. But Olly wasn't like most boys. He had never felt this way about a girl before and Emm had already spoken the most words to him of any girl who was not a blood relation. She was already in the record books on that one and it took her one day. So Olly smiled warmly and innocently at Emm when she offered 'good friend' to him. Olly tried to feel glad that she would at least be his friend. He could feel the metal squeezing his heart again. Olly didn't care. He went for it.

"So will you come to the prom with me?" he asked, straddling the line between courage and idiocy. "As my friend?"

Emm looked into his eyes. "Olly," she said as gently as she could, "I'm not ready for public displays of Michael Jackson."

Olly nodded at her. The metal bars tightened around his heart like a boa constrictor. Olly refused to express the pain on his face.

John was already at the edge of Old Man Johnson's well when Emm and Olly got there. The well was circular and made of centuries-old grey stones. It had a peaked roof and everything. *Your classic fairy tale well,* Emm thought. She unscrewed the lid to the crystal water bottle and then froze. *What am I doing? What if Old Man Johnson lives in the well or something? I can't do this.* She peered over the lip of the well, but all she could see was darkness. It was hard to tell if there was even water down there. Or old men.

"Come on, let's go. Do it." John said.

"Do what? There's no water."

Olly looked beneath the roof. "No bucket on a rope..." He leaned over and peered down the black cylinder. Then Olly barked like a dog... a dog that could fit in a purse. "Yip!" Emm and John looked at him like he had lost his mind.

"Yip! Yip!"

"Hardly an echo," Olly explained, "so there's probably water down there, a little further than we can see."

John looked for himself. He squinted.

"I think I see it," John said. "I can reach that. Pass me the bottle."

Emm glanced at the last rays of the sun in the sky as she passed John the crystal bottle. "The sun's almost down. Hurry."

John looked back and down at Olly. "Maybe grab my feet... you know, just in case," John said.

"You think I'm gonna keep you from falling in? You're like two hundred pounds!"

"Two forty," John said, and he bent over into the well and stretched his arms as far down as they would go. It was tough to see in the darkness, but John used all of his frame. Emm grabbed one of John's legs to help Olly. Olly needed the help as John's feet left the ground. Olly and Emm dug their feet into the ground and leaned all the way back as John's knees went over the lip of the well.

"God, you're heavy," Olly growled.

"Couple more inches," John shouted back. He dropped down a little further... a little further still... John still wriggled and got lower. "Come on," John growled through clenched teeth. Emm could feel herself losing her grip.

"Hurry up," she said desperately.

Emm peeked over the edge of the well as the sun disappeared over the horizon, leaving them enveloped in the blue of twilight. For just a millisecond, she could have sworn that the pale blue light of dusk reflected on some water down there, and as soon as that millisecond came and went:

SPLASH-SNAP

Something in the water leaped out, or seemed to leap out. The water geysered up like it was possessed by some kind of being; a demonic dolphin leaping from the depths, into the air, and back down again. Water sprayed up over the edge of the well and got in Emm's hair.

The millisecond after that millisecond, John started to flounder like a lunatic and screech, "Agh! Pull me up! Pull me up! Oh god!"

Olly pulled but Emm needed to help before John finally slid up and out, flumping on the ground like dead fish. He was soaked from head to toe and almost passed out. Water sprayed off of John's lip as he gasped and panted. "Something," John said between wet gasps, "something took the bottle."

"Something took your whole hand," Olly said.

"Huh?"

John raised the arm that held the bottle. Raised it up to his face.

No hand.

There was no blood or gore or anything – just a stump where his hand was. It was more than enough to make John freak right out. He let a bloodcurdling scream loose that echoed into the well itself. He gasped and screamed again. John was losing his mind as quickly as he had lost his hand.

"He needs a doctor," Emm said between John's screams, "help me get him up."

As Olly reached down, another splash came from the well. An object flew out of the well with a spray, over Olly's head, left him drenched, and landed in the grass a couple of yards in front of them.

It was the Crystahll Couture Water Vessel. And it was full of water, with the lid firmly screwed in place.

"What the what?" Olly said.

As soon as John clapped eyes on the bottle, something came over him. He instantly stopped screaming, stood bolt upright and reached for the bottle with his one remaining hand.

"I need a drink," John said and stopped them from pulling him.

"You need a hospital," Emm said.

"I'm going into shock and I need a drink of water," he insisted.

Olly grabbed the bottle, twisted off the cap and looked inside. It looked like water.

He handed the bottle to John, who took a swig so heavy it was like John had spent a week in the desert. Jonhn gulped until he choked on the water. Emm had to pull the bottle away.

"Ah," John said. Then John convulsed and fell to his knees. From the stump where John's other hand had once been, a grey mass blossomed out, defying gravity and chemistry and logic all at the same time, and began to take a grey metallic shape and shot into five metal digits. When the flowing and waving stopped, John sported a brand new iron hand, thicker and larger than his previous hand, but just as flexible. He wiggled his new fingers to test it out.

"Much better," John said, as though he hadn't been screaming out in mortal agony just seconds earlier. "I feel totally great! Like I just drank four energy drinks!"

"Did your wish come true? What did you wish for?"

"Wait," Olly said. "You couldn't possibly have wished for that..."

John shook his head, happily, then used his new metal hand to point at Olly and say "you are correct. Yes!" He gave Olly a metal thumbs-up. Then John stared into the palm for a moment. "You know, maybe if my wish can't come true, maybe I get what I need instead. "

"You need a metal hand?" Emm said.

"To beat the crap out of Prince Charming," John said. "He pulled a knife on me, you know that? Well take this, you British jerko!" He karate chopped the air with his new hand.

"I think I'm thirsty," Olly said.

"Take a hike." Emm tucked the bottle into her armpit. "Obviously the magic water got him buzzed a little bit."

"Oh my god," John interrupted. "I can't fly in a plane ever again."

"Metal detectors." Then John shrugged and headed back to the car.

25

John was giddy and overexcited all the way to the shopping mall, driving like a maniac and running up the curbs, but it seemed to be wearing off by the time they reached the parking lot and his speed had become almost acceptable. Thankfully, no one got killed. They got into the mall just as it was about to close.

Lights turned off and security doors roared as they slid shut. As Emm, Olly and John jogged past TGI Friday's, two girls with Hello Kitty purses pounded their fists on the doors, but a hostess inside just stood there, shaking her head at them, mouthing 'we're closed.' Even to the most obtuse, retail-addicted teen, the mall was clearly and obviously shut down for the night.

Except for Spindle.

Emm had hoped they would get there before Spindle shut its doors for the night, but as they rushed to the top of the escalators and looked down the corridor, it became clear that Spindle was not going to shut down for the night – and maybe not ever. The place was still packed. The dance music still thrummed. Girls still lined up, four wide, more girls now than in the middle of the afternoon.

The security guard recognized them immediately and waved them through, speaking through his headset to someone on the inside. Girls clamored for their purses and glass slippers and frog-kissing lipstick like they wouldn't be on sale tomorrow. Another zombified girl – this one just twelve, at the oldest – staggered past as they made their way to the cash registers. *Another one*, Emm thought. *Am I crazy for doing this?*

A woman old enough to be Emm's mom grabbed her by the shoulders. The woman had a crazy look in her eyes; a desperate look.

"Do you have a key? How do I get a key?" the woman said.

John pushed the woman aside. "You don't want one," he said, and they made their way to the cash registers at the back.

Emm slammed the filled Crystahll Couture Water Vessel down on the counter and Banana-Nose spun to face them, clearly startled. The thin old man was startled, too: he nearly leapt two feet in the air on the sound of the water bottle slamming down.

"How come no one ever buys anything here?" Olly said as Banana-Nose clutched her side, recovering from the startle.

"We're not that kind of store," Banana-Nose said. A look of worry crossed her face as she spied John's new iron appendage.

Emm pointed at the list:

1) Wear the Oro Fleece Poncho,
2) Drink from the Crystahll Couture Water Vessel,
3) Apply the Skin Deep Beauty Ointment.

"Ointment," Emm said. *I have to find out. I have to see for myself.*

"What's the rush?" Banana-Nose said. "What's the rush? Come back tomorrow, dearies."

"No. We see Mavis and stop this right now."

"You're not going to like what you see. Not going to like it."

"Sometimes you suck a lemon to get to the lemon meringue pie."

Banana-Nose shrugged. "Fine. Go. See what you see."

"Fine."

So they did. They marched up to the velvet rope and Emm stepped right over without hesitation. John and Olly followed suit, but not quite so self-assured, since they had both become partly metallic. Banana-Nose crept up behind them.

I'm giving this lady a piece of my mind. Emm whipped open the curtain and, to her complete disbelief, was met with nothing but a solid brick wall. *I've seen Mavis's face behind this curtain. I've seen girls walk out of a room behind this curtain!*

"All in good time," Banana-Nose said. "Now isn't the time. Tomorrow. Yes, tomorrow. Maybe you don't want to go any further anyway, deary?"

Emm was incensed. Like steam-in-the-nostrils incensed. "I am going to save my friends here and everyone else you crazy people have wrecked."

"Maybe they don't want saving."

"Just show me the ointment."

"You can't..."

"I can!" Emm roared. "I can do anything. Even if it sucks as bad as this sucks."

Something softened in Banana-Nose's baggy, wrinkled eyes – something that looked to Emm like surrender. Maybe even disappointment. Either way, Banana-Nose raised a gnarled finger to point at a display case near the front of the store.

"Let's go," Emm said and they moved out.

Banana-Nose grabbed Emm by the shoulder as they walked away. "Wait," Banana-Nose said, but something was different in her voice. "Is this what you really want?"

"I think... I think this is what I'm here to do," Emm said, realizing it as she said it. There was something about this that felt like she ought to be doing what she was doing. *I am where I'm supposed to be, right here, right now. I finally found somewhere I belong. And it's in the middle of this hellhole. So what exactly does that say about me?*

Banana-Nose got closer to Emm's ear and said something softly:

"Nothing will bring your father back."

Emm staggered back in shock. *What does she know about Dad?*

"Come see me when it's done, deary!" Banana-Nose shouted with a lilting crackle, as though Banana-Nose hadn't just dropped a bomb in Emm's ear. "Come see me."

Emm staggered to the display case, trying to shake the words out of her hair.

"Please," Banana-Nose said to herself, under her breath.

At the display case, only one tube of Skin Deep Beauty Ointment sat on the shelf. It was the largest lotion tube ever manufactured, spectrum-colored and maybe two feet tall. Olly and John stared at it like the tube itself was magical. Emm regained her composure and walked between them. "Last bottle," Olly said.

It was just then that the ginger kid walked right in front of them, snatched the last bottle of ointment from the shelf, and made much ado of taking it away from them.

26

He appeared to be about seventeen, with rusty-red hair that flowed and waved like a wheat field in the wind at sunset. He had a raccoon's mask of freckles and yellowing skin, and had to yank up his oversized jeans to cover his butt. At the same time, the ginger kid waved the bottle of ointment as he walked away.

"Dibs," the boy said.

"Hey! We need that," John called.

"How bad you want it?" the kid called back, a devious grin crossing his face. Emm, John and Olly took one step in pursuit – and the boy held his hand out to stop them.

"Whoa," he said with authority. "Let's not get hurt here." And with that, he started in on a twisting callisthenic variant of a jumping jack. "Gotta get loose before a run," he winked. Emm felt a growl bubbling up in her throat. Just as she pounced, the red hair took off, ointment held high in the air, a gleeful laugh finding its way to Emm's ears. That made her even more ticked.

The kid who just stole their ointment bowled over a couple of zombie girls before he got out of the store. They seemed to get just close enough to grab him, but somehow their hands never touched him. The kid twisted and ducked and hurdled at exactly the right time. Every time.

"Who is this guy?" Emm said to Olly, breathless.

"Lucky!" The boy called back to her. "Lucky Miller!"

"Well, don't be a d-bag, Lucky Miller. We need that ointment."

"Good luck catching me," Lucky Miller said.

John gave up. One thing John wasn't was quick. He stopped and bent over as he admitted to himself that he would never catch up to them. But John didn't admit defeat.

Olly took another shot at Lucky. He beared down a little more and sprinted a little faster, then reached to tackle Lucky with both arms. It was hopeless. Lucky chose that moment to slow down and let Olly olé right past him and take a tumble. Lucky turned and backpedaled beside Emm.

"Aren't ya gonna tell me *your* name?" Lucky said with a flirtatious smirk.

"No," Emm said.

"Let me guess... starts with an M. No – Emily. Emm."

The surprise was enough to make Emm stop running. Lucky continued to the escalator.

"How did you –"

"Lucky guess." He reached the escalator down. With his back still to it, Lucky tossed the bottle of ointment behind him, over his shoulder, down to the main floor. That made Emm's eyes bulge. But when Lucky Miller did a reverse swan dive backwards out of sight, it made her run terrified to where he had been just a moment ago. Olly and Emm reached the top of the escalators at the same time. They looked over the edge and there was

Lucky, at the bottom, on his feet, the ointment in his hand.

"Give up?" Lucky called.

"We can't, you jackhole!" Olly shouted back. Then they spied John, who snuck up behind Lucky to lay an iron-handed haymaker on Lucky's ear. Except Lucky had the good fortune to scratch his knee at the precise moment John's metal maw whooshed overhead, and Lucky avoided the punch.

"*You* drank the water?" Lucky said as he saw the metal fingers. But Lucky didn't wait for an answer. Instead, he took off once again. John looked up at the other two and shrugged.

"What do we do?" Olly said to Emm.

"We're done," Emm said, defeated. "Come up," she called to John. "We're done."

27

They went back to Spindle and searched for more ointment but came up empty. They went to the cash registers and asked the thin old man for help, but the thin old man just went to find Banana-Nose and Banana-Nose seemed pleased that there was no other choice but to give up.

"I admire your pluck, but you'll have to wait for next shipment," Banana-Nose cackled.

"When's the next shipment?"

"Weeks, surely. Weeks. Off to school with you three!"

"We're not leaving."

The security guard walked up to the desk and folded his arms.

"Yes you are," Banana-Nose said.

John got ready to fight, but Emm urged him away. They made for the parking lot, defeated.

"I'll never save Jessica," John said as they walked through the parking lot to the car. "She's gonna be like that for the rest of her life. Maybe she'll marry that guy."

"Um hello? I have a cage around a major internal organ. What are we doing about that?"

"I'm always gonna be a freak," Emm said.

"Oh, your problems are so terrible," John sneered.

"Have some perspective, Emm," Olly said. "You wanna be a freak or you wanna be a zombie? I mean, we need answers here, but maybe sending you into the zombie-making machine wasn't the best idea to begin with."

But Emm was so sure that was what she was meant to do. "I don't know anymore," she murmured. Maybe she did want to be a zombie after all, just like all the preppie trend-followers who wished they were princesses. Maybe, after it was all said and done, maybe Emm wanted to be a princess too. *Freak or a zombie... what's the difference?*

"If you weren't a freak," Lucky said from behind them, "you wouldn't be in this mess, Emm."

John readied his fist and relished the thought of putting it through this kid's face.

"Whoa, whoa, easy there, Loyal John," Lucky said. "Here." He offered Emm the bottle of ointment.

"I had to get you out of there," Lucky said, "so we could talk."

"You know what? Keep it," Emm said through gritted teeth. "Maybe it'll help with your freckles." She put a little extra emffffasis on the f in freckles. Then she tried to walk away.

Lucky just snickered, like she wasn't trying to be clever at his expense. "I can see why they picked you."

"Picked you for what?" Olly said.

"Just my luck. You guys are totally clueless still."

"Can I punch him now?" John polished his metal fist.

Lucky Miller took Emm's hand and brought her a little closer to him. He spoke gently to her and she felt something... different about him. Good different. Attraction, she thought.

Hotness. "You're the only one who can stop all this craziness, Emm," Lucky said softly, "You have a day and half. Two days if you're – you know." Lucky placed the ointment in Emm's hand like it was a single red rose. Emm felt the blood rush to her cheeks and her head felt like she was falling from a high, high place. *So this is what it feels like*, she thought.

Olly reached for his heart-cage and grimaced to himself.

"Never forget who we are, Emm," Lucky said.

"What is up with people knowing my father's last words?"

"You need to understand," Lucky said.

"No, *you* need to understand how creepy that is!"

"What's your deal, Carrot-Top," John barked.

"Real original," Lucky said, then turned back to Emm. "Emm, you have been chosen to protect the stories of the people whose stories... erm... are odd. The people who don't want to be like everyone else. The stories of a shrinking minority."

"Whatnow?" Olly said. Emm was too puzzled to do or say anything.

"You *are* a freak, Emm. You are. And now you're about to be the champion of freaks everywhere. You and your two brothers-in-arms, here."

John didn't appear to be taking it as a compliment. "I just want my damn girlfriend back."

Lucky tutted and shook his head. "Too late for your girlfriend," he said. "She's the first of hundreds. Maybe thousands."

John's anger melted away to sadness. "But I have to

help..." he pleaded.

Lucky pulled out a pack of cigarettes and lit himself a smoke. "Listen, tin man," Lucky sucked in the cancerous smoke and held it in his lungs, "once you decided to give Emm a hand... well... that hand was meant for her. " Lucky turned his attention to Olly. "You," Lucky said, but Olly already knew. Olly tapped on his heart cage.

"She was supposed to..." Olly began, and they all knew the answer. The magic of the Spindle accessories was supposed to be for Emm. John and Olly had inadvertently taken them away from Emm. "It was getting me ready for The Alcove," Emm said as she discovered it.

"Maybe you guys have a chance to stop what's coming if the three of you stick together," Lucky said. "Maybe."

"How do we stop what's coming?" Emm said.

"The ointment will get you into The Alcove," he told Emm, his green eyes peering deeply into hers. "Find the tallest hill you can and at sunrise, put the ointment on." Lucky poked Emm in the chest. "You," he poked. "*You* put the ointment on. Keep it away from the Tin Man and Toto over here."

"We get it, we get it," Olly said.

Lucky began to walk away, back into the night's shadows. "Once it's done, get back here. If you're lucky, I'll be here to help you the rest of the way."

"Wait," Emm said. "Where do I put the ointment? All over? Or..."

Lucky came back to her and looked her up and down. "Here's good," he hummed gently and kissed Emm on the cheek. Emm felt weak in the knees and so did Olly – he keeled over in agony, crying out.

"Jealous much?" Lucky said. Emm and John tended to Olly

right away, and when Emm glanced up to see where Lucky had gone, he had completely disappeared.

"Stop trying to make my heart explode!" Olly screamed at Emm.

John pulled Olly up before Olly was ready. "Enough of this," John spat.

"It all stops now."

And with that, he stormed to the car. Emm followed John as quickly as she could, and wasn't trying to avoid Olly at all. At least that's what she told herself. Despite having a small heart attack as his aortas knocked against a magical metal cage, Olly made his way to the car, too.

28

John pulled his red convertible up to Jessica's house, which of course was a huge cookie-cutter minimansion on a cul-de-sac where every driveway had a basketball net, a Beamer outside the garage, or both. There may as well have been a turret that Jessica could have lived at the top of, Emm thought. Maybe a moat. They said people tried to keep up with the Joneses. These were the Joneses to whom they were referring.

"We got til sunrise for your skin thing," John said. "So I'm gonna make sure you never need to even try it."

"I don't really want a metal face," Emm said.

"Lucky said Jessica was the first of many. Well maybe she'll be the first of many to be saved. I know she wants to be saved. I know it."

"You're sure you want to do this," Emm said.

"I have to. She's my girl. Even if she was kinda shallow and mean, she was with me. And I don't let people down. Ever."

"You love her," Emm said.

"Maybe. I dunno," John scratched his nose.

"Loyal John is a good name for you," Emm said.

"Umm, guys?" Olly said from the back seat. He had been laying in the back seat, but the heart pain had let up enough that he could get up to a sitting position. And now he gestured at Jessica's front door. "The front door's open," Olly said.

"It wasn't open before," John said. He got out of the car.

The door was wide open, letting the light from Jessica's foyer spill out onto the grass. Someone was home. And someone must have seen them from the front door. John knocked on the door frame and called out: "hello? Mister Missus Jones?"

No answer. John crept in.

Olly did not creep in. He was frozen in place. Emm had to push him in with a shove and Olly stumbled through the doorway angrily.

"No nervous jokes?" Emm said.

"There are zombies in this house. Not funny."

Emm was just as afraid and creeped out as Olly was but she hid it a little better.

"Hello? Fairy tale zombie squad calling," Emm said.

"My zombie apocalypse kit. Dammit!" Olly whispered to her.

"Good point. I'd feel more comfy if I had a hatchet in my hand."

John shushed them with a single silent finger. He walked stealthily into the kitchen. Food was strewn all over the place. It looked like the insides of a stomach, with noodles, ripped-up pizza boxes with pizza still in it, an exploded bottle of soda, cheese used like some kind of primal paint over the cabinets. Drawers and cupboard doors were opened, some emptied on the floor.

John sniffed and wretched. "What is that stink?"

"Oh my god," Emm said, as she looked into the dining room, just past the kitchen. Mr. and Mrs. Jones sat there, as though they were about to tuck into to a delicious bowl of soup. Except there were bloody puncture wounds in their chests, where their hearts used to be. They had very literally been given chest cavities. Emm could see the lovely upholstery on the back of the dining room chair if she looked into Mr. Jones's chest. Mr. and Mrs. Jones looked like they took a lot of vacations, Emm thought. They were tanned, almost to the point where their faces were getting leathery. There were smile lines. Mr. Jones had worn a three-piece suit to dinner. Mrs. Jones had bazoombas that nearly spilled over the cups of her push-up bra. A fly took off from the top of Mrs. Jones's breast and flew right into the hole where Mr. Jones's heart used to beat.

"No, no, no..." John said, covering his mouth. He rushed into the dining room and reached out to touch them, then thought better of it. He ran his hand through his hair. And clanged his metal hand against his own skull. John turned to Emm. "You don't think Jessica... oh, god, Jess."

Olly strode into the dining room with a butcher's knife in one hand and a santoku knife in another. He casually handed the butcher's knife to Emm, who was in the middle of a dry heave.

"A zombie won't stop until the head is separated from the body," Olly said. "So we need to separate the head from the body."

"No one is hurting Jessica," John said.

"Clearly she is not Jessica anymore, John!" Emm could not contain the horror now. It was not just about fitting in and boyfriends and girlfriends and high school. Now it was life and death. Now it was a horror movie. "She killed her parents! Maybe ate their hearts. A human being couldn't do this, John."

And as though it was on cue, Prince Charming walked around the corner, bloody dagger drawn, boots making a clomping sound on the hardwood.

"Milady did not kill anyone," he told John as he admired the bloody tip of his blade. "Not yet. She was not ready until she hath et on their hearts, and alas, verily, the royal thirst for blood hath arrived." Prince Charming then became distracted by a fly, which buzzed around the bloodstained hole beneath Mrs. Jones's breasts. A look of "yum" made the Prince's eyes fill with a glow – and then his tongue darted out a full yard and snapped up the fly.

"Put that sword down and fight me like a man," John said, despite what he had just seen.

"I'm no man," Charming confirmed. "I'm Prince Charming. It's not me you want, anyway. Kkkkkk."

Jessica's answer was "kkkkkk" as she zombie-sidled into the dining room. Her face was covered in blood from her meal of parent hearts. Olly immediate got into a ready position, knife poised to kill Jessica if Olly got the chance.

Jessica growled like some kind of wild animal. She was less robotic than she used to be, but that just made her more terrifying to Emm.

"Separate the head from the body," Olly told Emm as she brought her knife up.

"No!" John cried. "Babe, look at me," he pleaded to Jessica, "it's me. It's Johnnie."

But Jessica growled in response and took a swipe at

John, who had to jump back to avoid a nasty scratch to the face.

"It appears milady has an insatiable appetite," Prince Charming said to John with a grin.

That was the last straw for Loyal John Rockwell. "That's *it!*" he declared, and launched his metal hand at Charming, flying right past Jessica. Charming nonchalantly raised the point of his dagger about two inches, fully expecting lumbering John to simply impale himself on it as he arrived to throttle the prince. Instead, John grabbed at the blade and pulled it with his metal hand. Charming held on as John tried to yank the dagger right out of his hand. Prince Charming pulled back and they locked in a tug-of-war for the dagger, spinning in circles, colliding with the dining room table and knocking the corpses to the floor.

As John's disgust momentarily distracted him, Prince Charming pushed John back and the two metals made sparks as the blade slipped out of John's hand.

"John!" Emm said as Prince Charming leapt up at John with agility of, well, a frog, and forced John down by landing on John's shoulders.

"Ugh," Prince Charming grunted as he came to land atop John's prone body. Prince Charming's eyes bulged. There was a flash of reddish light and then Prince Charming was gone, and in his place were the splattered entrails of a frog, dripped all over John's body. He wiped frog tongue off of his face with his fleshy hand while his metal hand held up the dagger he had somehow wrenched from Charming's hand. John hyperventilated.

"Guess he was a frog prince," Emm said.

Jessica broke out in a blood-curdling scream as she saw what happened. Olly and Emm covered their ears, but John immediately got up and rushed to her aid. She screamed and screamed and screamed, a supernaturally awful scream. John took her by the shoulders and shook her, but she would not stop. She also wouldn't look at John, instead staring at the fremains of her dead prince.

Olly gave John the throat-slash gesture with his finger across his throat. John ignored it and shook Jessica again. Then John got an idea. He looked at the tarnished tiara on her head, let go of Jessica's shoulders, and removed the crown.

29

The screaming stopped.

"Jessica?" John tried.

Her lipped twitched.

"She's still a zombie," Olly said before Emm shushed him.

"Jess, baby it's me. Please be okay."

Slowly, Jessica's eyes began to fill with life. Her hand trembled as it rose up to touch John's face with anything but certainty. John closed his eyes tearfully waited for her touch.

It never came. He opened his eyes.

Her fingers reached for the blood that soaked her chin. She looked down at her fingers, then over to her parents' corpses on the floor. Jessica Jones shook her head, at first slowly, then harder, as she remembered everything that had happened when she was a princess zombie.

"Ew," Jessica said. It wasn't a snobby ew. It was the only way a girl like Jessica Jones could communicate that something really truly awful had happened and please bring back her mother and father and there was no way she could live with what she had just done. She could only utter the one syllable, but ew said it all. She held her hands out like they were really, really dirty.

John didn't know what to do, except let a single steaming tear bulge out and drop from his eye.

"It wasn't you," Emm said. "It's not your fault."

Jessica slowly turned her head toward Olly.

"S-separate... the head... from the body..." she told him. She reached up above her head, where John was still holding the tiara, and Jessica took it away from him. She finally locked eyes with John and he thought it was more than he could bear. "Don't... let me down..." she whispered to John. And John knew he could never let her down, even in this nightmare hell moment. John did not let anyone down ever. He tried with every fibre of his being to stop his head from nodding yes, but he failed. Loyal John had promised to do it.

Jessica nodded back at John. Then she let the tiara slip out of her fingers and back onto her head. With the tiara resting on her head once more, she immediately began to twitch, as though her brain was being electrocuted by the tiara itself. All the life fled from her eyes once again. The room was completely still for a moment.

Then Jessica's head snapped over to Emm and her monstrous voice crackled, "I wear the slipper, bitch!"

"Run," Olly said. He grabbed Emm by the hand and pulled her out of the dining room, just as Jessica made a leap for Emm's heart. Zombie Jessica missed by an inch, falling belly-first onto the floor.

John landed on Jessica's back and pinned her to the floor with his knees. He held the dagger up with both hands and looked up at Emm.

"Leave," John said.

"Don't. We'll just lock her in here," Emm pleaded.

But John just shook his head. "I never let people down. Ever."

"Come on!" Olly tugged at Emm's hand and pulled her out of the cookie-cutter minimansion, where Loyal John did the unthinkable to prove his loyalty to the one he loved. As they caught their breath, Emm and Olly heard a crash and a roar from inside the house.

Then a moist slashing sound.

Then silence.

After a while, John walked into the front doorway, the light from the kitchen and foyer casting him in silhouette. The silhouette dropped Prince Charming's dagger to the floor.

John's voice sounded low and empty when he spoke. "What happens now," he said.

"We prepare for the zombie princess apocalypse," Olly said. "And then we fut shick up."

30

Olly still had the components of his zombie survival kit collected in his garage, where he had taken the picture he had used for his Earth Sciences presentation. That all seemed like such a distant memory now, since John's girlfriend had gone zombie princess and murdered her parents and then begged John to put her out of her misery. These types of things tended to make school memories feel distant.

John didn't say a word as he drove. Didn't look anywhere but on the road. Emm and Olly didn't even try to get him to snap out of it. There was a heaviness in the air now. Emm thought maybe things had changed forever and that the heaviness in the air was here to stay. It made the air feel even heavier.

Olly's house was way nicer than Emm imagined it would be. She imagined he would have lived in a house that was as tiny and run-down, just like hers was, but it was the typical Modesta McMansion: brown siding, two stories, a double-garage and a basketball hoop in the driveway. The basketball hoop looked brand new and never used, though. As Olly ran down the driveway with his backpack full of gear, a woman poked her head out of the front door. Emm assumed it was Olly's mom, though she seemed a bit old.

"You little bastard," the woman croaked. Olly hurried his walk. "Get back here!"

Olly flung the backpack into the car and yelled without looking back: "Got something I need to do, mom. I'll be home after you pass out."

The woman marched out of her house, showing no signs of drunkenness, as Olly hopped into the car. She had a flowery terrycloth nightgown on and it was worn and stained. Maybe the outside of the house was perfect, but Emm started to wonder about the inside.

"Drive," Olly said to John, but John didn't go anywhere. Mrs. Ford got close enough to reach into the back seat of the red convertible and pick Olly up by the ear. Which is what she did. Olly batted her hand away and Mrs. Ford started to slap him silly. Emm couldn't help but say "Mrs. Ford? Mrs. Ford!" as Olly and his mother slapped each others' hands. A wave of alcohol smell smacked Emm in the face. Mrs. Ford was very drunk.

Then Mrs. Ford got one good coast-to-coast slap on Olly. A big one. She cocked back, nearly back-handing Emm's face as she raised the hand above the shoulder, and then came down swiftly onto Olly's face, with a follow-through that equaled the arc of the initial backswing. Olly fell back into the seat of the car and reached for the spot one his jaw where his mother had hit him. John finally loosened his grip on the steering wheel. He was going to get up and protect Olly, Emm thought, and she was glad. Because she didn't know what to do right now. Her first urge was to scream at this terrible woman.

Mrs. Ford took a step back, as though someone else had slapped her boy's face. She reached forward, gently, not far enough to touch Olly, and she murmured what might have been the beginnings of "I'm sorry" before Olly screamed at her. "You drunk bitch!" Olly howled. "Leave me alone!" Olly began to cry. John opened his car door without looking at anyone or anything. Emm started to worry that he was going to murder Mrs. Ford.

"Mrs. Ford," Emm said with a nervous laugh, "things are very crazy right now, but we need to help some friends who are in trouble, okay? We need Olly's help." Emm glanced over at John, who was looking at his metal hand, still standing by his door. "We'll be back real soon, okay?"

Mrs. Ford's eyes bulged. She brought her face closer to Emm's, until her fiery whisky breath made Emm's eyes sting.

"You listen to me, you little strumpet," Mrs. Ford hissed. "I'll not have Oliver cavor- cavor- hanging around with whores at all hours of the night." Mrs. Ford was trying to say 'cavorting,' but she was too drunk to spit it out.

Emm had never been called a whore before and she couldn't help but get angry. "You don't even know me," she said to Mrs. Ford.

"Get us out of here," Olly told John, and John did as he was told.

"You leave, you won't come back you little bastard, if you know what's good for you." Mrs. Ford started to back up. Then she gave Emm the stink eye as she uttered one last curse at Olly: "I hope she doesn't give you Chlamydia."

As they drove away, Olly's mouth began to form an apology but a joke came out instead.

"Well," he said to Emm, "they say the girls you're

attracted to turn into your mother, so what does that say about you?"

This time, Emm just let it roll of her back. She was getting used to Olly's nervous jokes.

After a while, Emm said "Call me a whore" under her breath. Even just making the word made Emm's gut hurt. "Hey Mrs. Ford, I got a nice tiara for you, why don't you try it on?"

John looked over at Emm and she realized just how awful what she said must have sounded to him, what with the tiara's effect on his girlfriend. Before she could apologize, John's eyes bulged with a grim realization.

"What is it, John?" Emm said.

"I have a sister."

31

John sped through the streets of Modesta to get to his cul-de-sac.

"Margaret's nineteen," he said. "She just dropped out of college last week."

"You think she...?"

John could only half-shrug and half-shake his head. The possibility that his own parents were dead and that he would have to mercy-kill his sister was too horrible for him to ponder.

Emm started to worry about Steph. Sure, Steph was a little older, but Emm thought she was very pretty. She might even fall for something like a princess makeover. What if one of Steph's two jobs was at the mall? Emm felt selfish for never bothering to ask where Steph worked. Suddenly, Emm felt desperate to get back home. Plus she could retrieve her hatchets and put them to use.

Olly leaned forward. "John, if it's too late – "

"It won't be."

"If it's too late, I've got my weapons here. I will –"

"It won't be too late!"

The right tires of John's convertible left skidmarks

on his front lawn. They looked to the right and up, at John's sprawling home on the forested cul-de-sac, maybe the biggest home in town. And they all immediately realized it was too late. Windows were smashed in on each of the three floors. Lights blinked on and off in a couple of the rooms. The TV was on, but the channel was black and white snow.

"No..." was all John could say. Olly readied his backpack.

"It's okay, John. You don't have to do this," Olly said. Olly reached from his car door and John's arm whipped back and his metal hand clutched Olly's chest, holding Olly in his seat.

"I have to," John said. "Alone."

"If you go in there, I'm going in there, and you're supposed to protect me."

Emm put her hand on John's shoulder. "We're not going to find anything good in there, John."

They stared at each other until John let go, started his car back up, and peeled out around the cul-de-sac, waking the neighbors.

As they sped for Emm's house, John shouted into the air: "they'll be fine when I get home." And then John let himself break down, because he knew they would never be fine, and he would never be the same.

32

Emm slammed the front door of her house and called for Steph in a panic. Steph came out of the bathroom hurriedly, wiping her face with a towel.

"It's two in the morning!" Steph said. "Are you okay? Where have you been?"

"No time to talk – can you get my hatchets? I need my hatchets. I think I also need you to call the police."

"At two in the morning on a school night? What is going on, Emm? And what's with the poncho?" Emm almost forgot she was wearing it.

"All the cool kids are wearing this," Emm said.

"So you're doing what everyone else does now?"

"Steph? Hatchets?"

"I'm not doing anything until you tell me what is going on!"

"I'll explain everything as soon as you get my stuff," Emm said as she rushed into her bedroom and picked her backpack up from the floor. She turned it upside down and all of her schoolwork fell out of it. She didn't care. "Flashlight," Emm said to herself as she snapped her fingers.

"Flashlight... flashlight..." she said to herself as she whipped open the hall closet and rifled through it. Nothing.

"Flashlight... flashlight..." she said to herself as she rummaged through the cabinet beneath the bathroom sink. Then something registered in her brain and she slowly rose back up, just high enough to see over the bathroom counter and into the sink. *Did I really just see that?*

She really did just see it. Circling the drain was pinkish-grey makeup, mixed with water. The makeup-water circled a latex banana-shaped nose, which was stuck halfway down the drain. There was no mistaking it. It was Banana-Nose's banana nose.

The five-gallon plastic pail full of hatchets fell to the floor and startled Emm. "I can explain," Steph said from the bathroom doorway. Emm shot up and her nostrils flared with the rage of betrayal. "It's not what you think," Steph pleaded.

"You want me to be a zombie. That much is clear."

"No," Steph said. "I told you to come see me when it's done. *Before* Mavis."

Emm snickered to herself so that she wouldn't start crying. "I should have figured it out," Emm told Steph. "Fairy tale store. Zombie princesses. Wicked stepmother."

"No! Emm..."

"I thought we were running away from the freak show. But you were just taking us into a horror movie."

"You've got it wrong. Please. Wait."

But Emm just marched up to her, swiped the bucket of throwing hatchets, and left without another word. All that could be heard was the clanging of sixteen stainless steel hatchets in a five-gallon ice cream pail. They all clanged against Emm's knee with every angry step she took, which totally ruined her attempt at a classic melodramatic storm-off.

33

In the car, Olly and John were mired in a tense silence. Olly knew better than to even try and breach it with a joke – Olly wasn't nervous now, but he felt sick, like his nightmares were coming true and even if he wished for them to come true sometimes, it was making him sick now. The guy driving the car just killed his girlfriend. And it was a mercy killing. She asked him to do it. There was nothing to joke about there. Now his whole family looked like they were dead or worse. Olly took back all the times he wished his mom was dead.

Even though John punched Olly so hard it knocked him out yesterday, a lot had happened since then. Olly didn't have any friends, but now this guy, one of the top ten most popular dudes at school – heck, John probably goes to drinking parties – this guy had pledged never-ending allegiance to him. Plus they had both become the world's first cyborgs. Olly felt compelled to help his new... whatever this was.

"John." Olly started to reach for John's shoulder. But once the silence was broken, John snapped. He lurched forward and punched his windshield with his metal fist, making the safety glass shatter into a million shards. It made Olly jump back. John punched the windshield again and again until it fell away from the metal frame that held it.

And when John came to rest, Olly didn't dare break the silence again.

A chunk of safety glass held for a second, then fell to the dash with a clatter.

In tears, Emm kicked the ice cream pail with her knee and then let the momentum pull her across the front yard. With a sniffle, Emm reached the car and dumped the pail into the back seat beside Olly. Olly looked at her and frowned, but John sat perfectly still, eyes directly forward. Emm clocked what was left of the windshield. She forgot about her own pain and remembered what John had just done. Emm thought about touching his arm to comfort him.

"I couldn't let her down. Even..."

"You did the right thing."

John's head fell to the steering wheel. Emm carefully let her hand rest on John's back. John raised his hands up and looked at them - *what had they done? These hands? Murderer's hands.* Then Loyal John let himself grieve. His cry was angry and terrified at the same time, filled with so much pain that would have been equally fitting for someone who was having their leg amputated.

He raised his head and screamed at the stars. And then the anguish and fear left him. He turned to Emm with a steely look, as though he had been possessed by something.

"If you end up with a tiara on," John said, "I'll do the same to you."

"I know John. You'll never let me down."

John turned the key and stepped on the gas. Emm could feel Steph standing in the doorway, watching Emm drive away, but Emm didn't look back.

Then Steph got on the phone. "It's going down tonight," she said, and got ready to battle the zombie princess apocalypse.

34

The first rays of sunlight reached over the horizon like the yawning stretch of the recently awoken. But Emm, Olly and John hadn't slept all night. After Emm's house, they snuck into Olly's and gathered their zombie survival kits. Olly had some drive-thru, but Emm and John had zero appetite. For three hours, they gave each other shoves as they nearly dozed in John's car, waiting for the sun to rise over the tallest hill in Modesta. Hills, actually.

Kids (and some sophomoric adults) called the tallest hills in Modesta "the Parton hills," because they rose into the sky like two divinely-provenanced breasts, as though the world's most well-endowed country music entertainer was lying on her back, the hills rose high above, offering a view that went on for miles. At some point, in the days of eight track tapes, a man of poor taste looked at the hills and was reminded of the breasts belonging to well-endowed country singer Dolly Parton. The man of poor taste told other men of poor taste. The name stuck. Dolly Parton even visited the hills once and told all the men in town – who denied ever looking at Dolly Parton's breasts – how she appreciated being treated like royalty during her visit. Like a princess.

After some debate, John and Olly decided that the left mound was slightly taller than the right mound, and for that reason, they had driven to the top of the left Parton hill.

And waited.

For this moment.

"Here we go," Emm said, and stood up. She got out of the car and looked into the first second of dawn, then pulled out the gigantic, squeezable bottle of Skin Deep Beauty Ointment and squirted some into her hand. She looked around for a second, waiting to see if magical fireflies would swarm her hand, or if the ointment became a person-eating blob. Nothing.

She rubbed it into her arm. She was too afraid to do her cheek the way Lucky Miller had suggested. What if her face did indeed turn to metal? Or what if she got what she wished? Worse yet, what if she got what she needed?

Olly inspected her skin. "Is it supposed to glow or something?"

"Why, is it glowing?"

"You need to put it on your face," John said.

Ohmygod, he's saying my face needs ointment! There was a small part of Emm which realized this was not a typical thought that Emm would think. But that small part was getting smaller.

"Do I have a zit or something?" She obsessively rubbed the ointment into her forehead. "It's my nose, isn't it. Nose zits ohmygod." She rubbed it into her nose really hard.

Olly could tell something wasn't right. "Are you feeling okay?"

"Do I *look* okay. I can't have a zit. Does this look like a zit farm to you?"

"I think it's working," Olly said to John with a corked eyebrow.

"I don't see anything," John said and squinting at Emm like he was missing something.

That seemed to make Emm angry. "Are you saying I look plain? Then you have no taste, Moose, because hello, I am wearing an Oro Fleece Poncho from Spindle. People say I'm, like, prettier than Snow White. I say maybe I *am* Snow White but like modern and cool and stuff, so..."

"Oh, I get it," John said to Olly.

It actually was quite simple to get Emm into the car, once Olly figured it out. He just told Emm that Spindle was ready to give her the dream makeover she always wanted. Emm seemed to expect that, like it was about time, and she led them back to the car.

"I wonder what's going on in her brain right now," Olly said to John as they sped back to the mall. John looked into the rear-view mirror to spy on Emm. Her eyes weren't as vacant as J- (he couldn't bear to think of her name)'s but Emm was trying to look at her own hair by rolling her eyeballs up and back. John had seen some stoner kids at a party once, and that's exactly what Emm reminded him of. Totally unaware of how stupid they look. John wondered if he ever looked stupid to everyone else.

"I don't think much is going on in there at all," John said to Olly.

The car stopped outside the doors to the mall. It was a little after six in the morning – only custodians were there. "Nice job, Tiny. Now my hair is a total rat's nest," Emm scowled.

Lucky Miller walked around a corner, as though he had been waiting there all along. "Oh hey, nice timing," Lucky said.

"Get us in there," Emm ordered him. "I am having a hair catastrophe."

"What, in there? You mean like this?" Lucky hit the door with an elbow-elbow-heel-elbow-fist combo and the door swung open.

Emm pranced right through, completely forgetting about her zombie survival kit. John picked it up out of the car after he strapped his own over his shoulders. Olly had to bend over to keep upright with his massive pack. "Planning a camp-out?" Lucky said as they passed. Olly just gave him a dirty look and thought it was sufficient.

Lucky caught up to Olly as they moved toward Spindle. "Listen," Lucky said into Olly's ear, "she had to put the ointment on to get into The Alcove. It was like a test she needed to pass. Now I don't know about you, but I kinda liked her better before this whole makeover thing."

Olly didn't trust Lucky or Lucky's intentions but agreed with that statement. He let Lucky know with a reluctant nod.

"You got to make sure she doesn't lose her way completely, okay?"

"Who are you again?"

"I'm here to help you destroy the wish-granting zombie queen. Does that clear it up?"

It did not clear it up. Olly clenched his jaw a little more tightly than it was already clenched. *This guy needs a haircut,* Olly thought, *or some other kind of adjustment.* Olly remembered the way Emm looked at Lucky and it gave Olly's heart a little pang.

"Please, Olly," Lucky said, and his face actually registered sincerity for once, "don't let our little princess get too... princessy. Now I need to talk to Emm really... umm... intimately. You might want to look away for this next bit 'cuz of the heart thingie there."

Olly looked into Lucky's eyes and thought about popping them out of their sockets with his thumbs.

The lights were on at Spindle, but the security guard was nowhere to be found. They couldn't see anyone in the store, either. No music played. Spindle seemed open and abandoned. Lucky took Emm by the hands, and a jolt of pain shot through Olly's chest. He turned away as Lucky had asked.

"This is where I leave you," Lucky said. "Whatever happens during your makeover, don't wish for a tiara, okay?"

"Um, yah," she said like she was saying 'duh,' "who needs a crown when everyone knows you're royal?"

"Royal something," Olly mumbled to himself.

Lucky headed for the escalators and called out his final instructions. "Stay together as long as you can. When you get to the change room, you have to go it alone, Emm. Keep your heart pure."

"What does Emm do once she gets inside the change room?" John said.

"She fights the fairy tale."

"Oh, I'm not fighting," Emm said. "Not in this. This is not fighting wear."

"Good luck," Lucky said, and made another flying leap off of the second-floor railing.

35

Spindle looked like a department store looked at the end of Black Friday. Most of the fairy tale trinkets had been snatched from the shelves by would-be Cinderellas, Snow Whites, Jasmines, Rihannas, Sleeping Beauties, Belles, Kate Middletons, you name it. Olly wondered how many zombies there were now. John thought about how many girls were out murdering tonight, stolen away by frog princes who gave them the thirst for blood, just like J-(he couldn't bear to think of her name). Emm didn't think. She just bounded through the aisles, tra-la-la-ing her way to The Alcove. The velvet rope was unbuckled when she got there.

John could have swept the velvet curtain open, but he was mad. He yanked on it with his metal hand and tore the curtain right off the wall. Instead of the brick wall that was there before, the curtain revealed an ancient metal door, like the door to a dungeon, and that door had an ancient keyhole in it.

Emm pulled out her key and clapped giddily. "So excited!" She smiled ear-to-ear at Olly.

"Hello? Is Emm in there? Can I speak to her?" Emm was transfixed on The Alcove door. Olly looked up at

John.

"Remember what Lucky said," John scolded Emm. *Also remember what I said. You put on a tiara, I'll do it.*

Olly tried to look into Emm's eyes. He accidentally raised his voice, as though he were to calling to Emm over a long distance. "We're with you, Emm," he called, "keep you heart pure."

Emm didn't seem to care. She brushed herself off. "Let's see, I have my to-die-for poncho, my skin is absolutely radiant, and now I'm going to make my princess ensemble complete! Water, please." She held her hand out. Olly pulled the water bottle out of his pack and handed it to her.

He looked up at John. "It didn't work," Olly said. John violently pushed Emm up against the door.

"Remember what I said," John's voice boomed. "Remember what I will do if you put on a tiara. Remember? Remember?" He shook Emm until she nodded. She seemed to almost awaken for a moment.

"Right... right. Who would want that? Don't worry about me," she said. *You do. You want it.*

"You gotta fight it, Emm, or we're totally screwed."

"I will," she said. *But can I win the fight?*

Emm's hand trembled as she put the key in the lock and turned. With a rusty squeal, the door opened.

They saw a narrow room with grey stones and mildew and long candles in a row. At the back of The Alcove, sipping her tea, was Mavis Stiles. She luxuriated in a crimson Queen Victoria highback chair.

"Welcome to The Alcove," her raspy voice made Emm feel soothed. It put Olly on edge.

"I'm sorry but the key is for one person only," Mavis said.

"Oh, uh... they used some of your – products, too."

There was a pause before Mavis waved them inside. "Let's have a look at you, then."

They continued into The Alcove for a few more steps. John whispered "now?" to Olly and Olly whispered "patient." As they got near, Mavis stood up and straightened out her drop-dead-gorgeous little black number.

"I like your dress," Emm said. *Fight it fight it fight it.*

"Black absorbs the most light, did you know that? Now let's have a look at you." Mavis cupped Emm's chin and raised Emm's head. As Mavis peered into Emm's eyes, she said "something different about you..." and then, as though something clicked in Mavis's mind, she broke her stare and looked at the two boys.

"Sorry. One person per key." Mavis waved her free hand and sent the boys flying backwards, as though it was the easiest thing in the world to just wave your hand and send people flying backwards. John and Olly each flew through the doorway and right out of The Alcove. "Fight it, Emm," Olly yelled as he was repelled. The door slammed shut of its own accord.

Emm swallowed nervously as Mavis gazed into her eyes again. "Oh," Mavis said, "the princess we will make of you."

"You've been making a lot of princesses..."

"That's what we do here." Mavis started to inspect Emm like a tailor inspects an inseam. "We're making dreams come true. Working with my exclusive suppliers, I have the power to make your heart's stylistic desire become reality, and I want to share my fashion secret with every little girl who's ever wanted to be a princess.

A Snow White for you, I think. Haven't you always wanted to be Snow White?"

Emm struggled to find the words and she couldn't help but stammer. "N-never... occurred to m-me." The tiny voice in a dark corner of Emm's mind said *fight it,* but the voice was getting quieter.

"You know prom is tonight, yes? Show all the boys that you're the fairest in the land. Nice poncho."

"This? I got it from here... Oro Fleece."

Mavis scoffed. "That's from out front. The stuff out front is just window dressing. A teaser. Here is the main attraction." From behind her chair, Mavis pulled out the shiniest thing Emm had ever seen. Shinier than diamonds. Shinier than looking into a halogen light bulb. Maybe even shinier than the sun itself. The shiny thing was a tiara.

"You're tired of being like every other girl. You want to be noticed. Who doesn't? Who doesn't want to feel pretty?"

"Not me."

"Not anyone." Mavis offered Emm the tiara. Emm couldn't even look directly at it. "Why don't you go into the change room and try it on?"

Emm nodded, even though she felt like maybe she shouldn't nod. But she didn't take the tiara.

"Wait. What about Prince Charming?" The small part of Emm that was fighting got a little bigger.

"Yes, every princess needs her prince and we have that covered as well. In the change room. Why don't you go in there, Emm?"

Mavis opened the change room door and Emm looked inside. It looked like a very innocuous-looking change room, like a change room at JC Penney. Mavis tossed the tiara into the room and gestured for Emm to go in. Emm took a step or two.

"So," Emm thought aloud, "why does Prince Charming murder people? There's nothing very charming about that."

Mavis's face curdled. Any pretense of kindness evaporated from her. "I don't know what you mean," Mavis said flatly.

"My friend got one of your tiaras and Prince Charming showed up, murdered her parents and fed her their hearts. Thankfully my friend John killed him, but then he had to kill his own girlfriend because she begged him to do it. She couldn't live with what she had done. But what I don't understand," Emm said, now fully in control of her faculties again, "is why? What is the point?"

Mavis shoved Emm into the change room and Emm fell to her knees.

"The point is," Mavis said as she licked her teeth, "that every girl wants to be a princess. Even the oddest of oddities. Even you."

And with that, Mavis slammed the door shut. There was no handle to get back out.

36

Emm tried to pry the change room door open, but there wasn't even a crack to dig a fingertip into. It looked like a giant, mirrored wall, as though the door was never there to be begin with. Slowly, Emm turned around. She wasn't in a JC Penney change room anymore. This room was much, much larger. And much more frightening.

Every wall, the ceiling and floor, all of it – it was all covered in mirrors. Millions of Emm reflections looked back at her as she looked around, up, down. In fact, they were infinite Emms. She was looking into the infinite, and it looked back at her. Emm felt like she needed to get closer to them, like something was drawing her in. She tried to shake the feeling off.

At the center of the room, a circular stone object sat. It was grey and looked out of place. It almost looked like a circular couch, with a pedestal at its center. On top of the pedestal were two things: the way-too-shiny tiara, whose gleam shot into the mirrors and bounced all over the place, glowing more brightly than Olivia Newton John in Xanadu, if Emm had ever watched TV; and beside the tiara was what looked to be half of an oak barrel – the kind in which one might ferment wine. Even though it was only half a barrel, the barrel was big enough that it could have held a full barrelful of monkeys.

Emm crept toward the barrel to see what was inside.

Before she could get to the barrel, she thought she heard something behind her.

"Hello?"

Out of the corner of her eye, Emm could have sworn she saw a shadow moving between reflections in the mirrors. Like a shadow was flying around inside the mirrors. Emm didn't like that at all. She backed onto the stone couch and slid her back against the pedestal. She didn't move a muscle. She just wished she had her hatchets right now.

37

Outside the brick wall that used to be the door to The Alcove, John pounded and pounded to no avail. "I knew we should have attacked when we had the chance."

Olly crouched over his backpack and pulled out a metal spike with a hammer. He handed them to John. "Try this."

"Stop that this instant," said Banana-Nose as she approached the boys. The thin man followed close behind her. "Your friend will have to make do on her own."

"You can drop the old lady act, Mrs. Dillinger," Olly said. The thin man to start flailing his arms wildly, pantomiming 'shut up, shut up.'

Olly kept going. "It's disgusting – her own mother."

"She can hear you!" The thin old man growled.

"Run!" Steph said beneath her latex banana nose.

"I'm not leaving this spot," John said.

The thin man reached for his hair, pulled at it so hard that his latex mask came off. The silver facial hair of an aged Pedro the Wolf-Boy scared the living bejeebers out of John. Pedro roared like a wolf to make John run, but it was too late.

The stone wall exploded with a rumble, stones flying as

though the wall was fake. As though the Kool-Aid man was trying to walk through it. The stone rubble buried John, but Olly rolled away, hammer and spike still in hand. Mavis walked daintily through the hole.

"You had to do this while I'm wearing my best shoes," she cackled. Then she looked over at Pedro without his mask, and Banana-Nose, both of them in fighting stances. Mavis laughed. "You two? Note to self: don't trust reference checks."

Olly crawled on his belly toward Mavis, who continued to mock Pedro and Steph. "Clean up this mess or you're fired."

"We'll never let you win, Mavis."

"It's not win or lose, Dillinger. It just is. As we speak, your girl is inside –" Olly drove the spike into Mavis's foot and slammed the hammer down as hard as he could.

The spike, halfway into the floor and all the way through her foot, must have been painful. But Mavis didn't show it. She just looked down with an annoyed look on her face, removed the spike with two fingers, and then levitated Olly with an easy gesture.

"People stand when they face me," she said, and then made a sweeping motion with her hand.

Olly's legs twisted together like twine. The bones broke as they were forced to flex, snapping in a thousand places. Round and round they legs went, round each other, as Olly floated in the air, screaming in the excruciating throes of Mavis's magical torture.

Like a periscope, John's metal hand shot up from the rubble. He began to pull himself out. Steph, still wearing her latex nose, tried to distract Mavis before she saw

John. "Leave the Norms alone and fight us," Steph said, but it didn't work. Mavis watched as John got to his feet. With another casual wave of the hand, she released her grip on Olly, but his legs stayed intertwined.

"Norms?" Mavis said. "Half-norm at best." Then she realized who John was. "You're the one who killed his girlfriend." John didn't respond. He just took a step in her direction. "I'll bring her back. If you help me with my two employees of the month."

John stopped. He looked over at Steph and Pedro.

"It's a trick, Niño," Pedro said. "No wish can bring back the dead."

Steph took a step backward, fearful that John was about to turn on them. "Pedro is right. Please, if you care for Emm, take Olly and both of you get out of here."

Mavis crossed her arms and allowed this scene to entertain her. When Steph was finished her piece, Mavis turned to John and shrugged. "So? What's it gonna be?" John looked at all three of them, and Olly writhing on the floor, as they waited for his answer.

38

Emm sat on the stone couch and wondered when someone was going to rescue her. It felt like she had been waiting a long time already, and there was nothing to do but look at her own infinite reflections. They seemed to look uglier and uglier, the longer she looked at them. *No one is coming. No knight in shining armor is coming for this damsel in distress.*

Then she heard what sounded like a frog croaking. It came from the barrel, which towered above Emm's head. She never thought to look into it, since she had backed into the stone chair out of fear for whatever might have been moving inside the reflections of the mirror. Now Emm got up, climbed up onto the circular stone couch, and tiptoed to look into the half-barrel.

Sure enough, there was one frog in there. But the barrel was covered in froggy slime. At one point, the barrel might have held hundreds of frogs. Emm reached down to touch the frog – then a shadowy flash crossed her peripheral vision, making her spin around and call out: "hello?"

Emm heard what sounded like far-off whispering. She couldn't make out any distinct words, but she could tell it was a voice. "Hello, whisperer ghost. I can totally hear you whispering."

This time, across the reflections above her, she saw a shadowy figure, almost like black robes, float across, clearly into view and then quickly back out. "I saw you, Casper. Come on out." She left the frog alone and started walking closer to a wall, trying to catch the thing in the mirrors again. She got close enough to one mirror-wall to press her back to it. Emm looked over at the frog as it jumped over the edge of the barrel and onto the stone couch. Then she looked at the tiara, which seemed to shine brighter than light itself.

"Put it on," whispered the voice from behind her, inside the mirror. She gasped and spun around. Nothing was there but her own ugly face. Oh, how she hated it. Oh, how she needed that tiara to distract from it. After a valiant attempt at a comeback, the voice that told her to fight was now completely gone.

Emm walked back to the tiara. The frog watched her pick it up and close her eyes.

"Put it on," came the whisper, even louder now, from above.

Emm remembered Lucky's advice: "Keep your heart pure." *How can my heart be pure when I'm so... ugly.*

Her fingers brought the tiara to within an inch of her black curls.

Keep your heart pure. Keep your heart pure.

"Put it on."

Her fingers let go of the tiara and it touched Emm's head.

39

Loyal John, brandishing his metal fist, walked toward Mavis, who squared off against Pedro and Steph, waiting for John to join her.

"Once I'm on your team," John told Mavis, "I never stop fighting for you."

"I can give you everything your heart desires."

John took a tentative step toward Mavis.

"That's a good boy. Come closer."

John came even closer.

And then he cold-cocked Mavis across the cheek. It sent her reeling.

"Now!" Pedro shouted, and pounced, claws extended. Steph pulled out a pump bottle of sunscreen that was as big as fire extinguisher. She sprayed it at Mavis, coating her from head to toe. Mavis raised her hand to protect her face, but the sunscreen burned her flesh in every spot it landed.

John rushed to Olly and scooped him up from the ground. Olly couldn't let go of his twisted-up legs. The pain was making Olly veer in and out of consciousness.

Pedro landed on Mavis and clawed at her with his wolfen paws. They rolled around in a melee, with Mavis giving as good as she got, despite her skin smoking in places. Steph turned to John and screamed: "get out of here before she can do anything else to you!"

As though on cue, Mavis gestured and threw Pedro the Wolf-Boy across the store, through display cases and against the far wall. Pedro was unconscious before he hit the ground. With Olly in his arms, John got out of there in full sprint. Olly came to as they got into the shopping mall corridor.

"No! Emm!" Olly pleaded. They watched as Mavis rose to her feet and dusted herself off. Steph sprayed the sunscreen again and Mavis ducked.

"Oh, please," Mavis chortled. "You can't just turn off the sun."

"Watch me try, biatch," Steph said and sprayed Mavis's face. The skin bubbled and smoked, but Mavis did not flinch.

40

Emm examined her hands, then looked up to her the reflection in the mirror. A single reflection. Emm didn't realize it, but the infinite reflections were gone and now there was only one Emm staring back at her. She stared into her own eyes.

"I'm so ugly right now," she said, puffing her cheeks with air and pouting a clownish pout.

A face appeared in the mirror, as though just over Emm's reflection's shoulder, hovering, never quite staying still. A man's face.

It was the Amazing Derek Dillinger's face.

His eyes were gentle and they filled quickly with tears as he got his fill of his nearly-grown daughter. He passed his hand in front of her face for a moment as though he was checking for blindness.

Emm tried to look around him as she primped. "Stop it, Daddy, I'm trying to fix this mess here."

"Emily, look at me," her father said.

"If I look at you, I can't see myself, Daddy."

"Emm, where is your father right now?"

"He, like, died when I was – wait a minute."

Finally, she came to. Emm watched the life return to her own eyes, then finally saw who was speaking to her on the other side of the mirror.

"Daddy!" Emm cried and pressed her hand up against the mirror.

"There you are," Derek Dillinger said. "We haven't much time. Mavis will be here soon and she can't find out about me."

"I miss you so much. I will never take this off as long as I can see you. Things got so crazy..." She held her hand against the reflection as her father did the same, simulating a touch that neither of them could truly feel, wish though they might.

"No! You must take off the tiara the second that door opens. That barrel was full to the brim with frogs, which means there are two hundred Prince Charmings out there, at least. You need to take that last frog and destroy it when you get out of here. Then you need to get every last one of them before they turn this entire town into cannibal murderers."

"Two hundred Charmings... two hundred zombies," Emm said.

"Two hundred is just the beginning. They'll give Mavis more power, then they'll infect more and more people – not just girls – the wish can be weaker and weaker as she grows stronger and stronger. Until anyone who wears one of those tiaras could eat your heart out."

"Zombie princess apocalypse," Emm said to herself.

"You could call it that. So many people wish we live in a fairy tale world that the universe is reshaping itself into what *they* want. Except they don't know what they're wishing for. And *they* aren't *us*."

"It's the cold times, isn't it. The sun..."

But Emm's father wasn't paying attention. It was as though someone was talking to him from a place Emm couldn't see.

"It's time," Derek said. "I will always love you." He moved away from the mirror a little.

"No," Emm pleaded. "How do I get you out of here?"

"You don't. I had to bend some rules just to cross over like this. But you can't bring back the dead, Emm. Just be pure of heart and remember where magic lives." Derek Dillinger pointed at Emm's heart. "Remind your stepmother when you get a chance."

"Daddy..."

"Fight the fairy tale," he said, and then disappeared as though he were being sucked into a vacuum.

Emm screamed out and pounded the mirror with both fists. They did not shatter. The tiara fell from her head as she pounded, tears streaming down both cheeks.

"Everything all right in there?" Mavis called from The Alcove.

Emm wiped her tears. *Get yourself together. Everyone is counting on you.*

"Yeah," Emm said with a sniffle, "yeah, like, I'm sooo pretty with this crown on me." She silently stuck her tongue out and put the tiara back on. It didn't do anything. Emm could only see one reflection of herself.

"Grab your prince and come on out, sweetheart. I have a surprise for you." Emm knew she had to come out, and once she did come out, she had to be ready to fight. Her Daddy told her so. "Guh," Emm said to herself in frustration, walked over to the little frog who sat on the circular stone couch and scooped him up. "Poor little froggy," she said to it.

"Your makeover is complete, Princess Emily Dillinger of the Snow Whites," Mavis decreed, like a queen dubbing a new member of the royal family. The doorway magically reappeared where the mirror was and Mavis was visible again, sitting in her Queen Victoria highback chair, drinking tea.

Emm did her best zombie princess walk through the doorway and into The Alcove. She even made a little "Kkkkkk" sound.

41

As soon as Emm took one step into The Alcove, she saw Steph and Pedro on their knees to her left, bound and gagged with duct tape. She pretended not to care and continued her twitchy trudge, frog in hand. The frog hopped onto her shoulder – and then into the collar of her poncho. *Princess or no, this is disgusting,* Emm thought.

Mavis's skin was burnt and blemished by the sunscreen, Emm noticed as she got up close.

"Don't you look regal," Mavis said. All good salespeople paid such compliments to their marks as they tried on things. There was a regular, full-length mirror in the corner of The Alcove and Emm noticed, as she glanced into it, that the tiara didn't shine anymore. It was tarnished, just like Jessica's was. Emm didn't have to fake-twitch. The sensation of a slimy frog slithering and paddling around in Emm's shirt was enough to make her wig out like she had her finger in a light socket.

"Let's run a little test, shall we? I don't sense a wish to betray me, but one can't be sure with you Oddities. So yes, a little test." Steph struggled harder against her bonds as Mavis snapped her fingers.

The frog crawled out from Emm's shirt, sprung

onto the floor, and transformed into a black-haired Prince Charming before Emm's very eyes. *Really*, Emm thought, *so many girls wish for Prince Charming that Mavis can just grow a barrel full of them? Although if I was going to have a Prince Charming, oddly enough, I'd probably wish him to look like this... but maybe with red hair.*

"Kkkkkkk," Emm said.

"I have arrived!" Prince Charming declared gallantly.

"Feed your princess the hearts of her family."

"And bestow upon her the royal thirst for blood! Gladly, my Queen!" He drew his long, thin dagger. It was exactly the same as the other Prince Charming's dagger. He looked over at Steph. It was enough for Emm to give up the charade.

"Stop!" she cried.

Mavis looked down at her fingernails, disappointed. "I'm losing my touch," she said.

"I'll do it, all right? I'll be your zombie Snow White and I'll help you. Just let them go."

"Do you want to save your poor stepmother and her little dog, too?" Pedro didn't appreciate being referred to as a dog. He growled beneath the duct tape.

"Yes, please..."

"But do you *wish* it? With all your heart?"

Steph shook her head and murmured against the duct tape, making it buzz. Steph was pleading for Emm to say no and Emm realized it was the wishing part that was going to get her in trouble. But Emm nodded anyway.

"Yes, Mavis. I wish it with all my heart."

"Then we're in business. Back to the change room."

It was then that Mr. Blake flew into The Alcove wielding a two-handed battle axe over his head.

42

Mr. Blake was no longer wearing his school uniform. In fact, he sported a medieval combination of brown leather and platemail armor as he flew through the air toward Mavis, two-handed battle axe over his head.

The two-handed battle axe had little tiny jewels encrusted in its handle and the back of the blade; each jewel was a different shape and size, but they all were a milky opal white. It didn't occur to Emm right then and there, because a lot of other things were occurring to Emm at the moment, but the jewels in Mr. Blake's battle axe were the same type of milky opal as Emm's heart-shaped necklace.

The main reason Emm didn't make this connection in her mind was because her guidance counselor was flying through the air in Lord of The Rings armor and performing a two-handed axe smash into the head of Prince Charming.

The axe slammed through Charming so hard he didn't have a chance to defend himself. The blade cut quick and clean and, with the same flash of light as the first Prince Charming, this one became a heap of frog parts as soon as the axe split him in two.

Mavis sucked on her tooth, unimpressed. "And which dwarf are you?"

"Smashy," Mr. Blake said, wiping frog from his face.

Emm sprung into action. She took the tiara off her head and threw it like a Frisbee at Mavis, who threw her hands up instinctively to protect her face. Mr. Blake spun his axe around so that the blunt jeweled side struck Mavis on her hip. The jewels seemed to glow a milky-white glow, like a full moon, as they made impact with Mavis's side.

Mavis fell to the floor, clearly hurt by the axe and its stones. Mr. Blake looked up at Emm, still wielding his axe in a ready position. "Moonstone," he said. "Won't keep her down very long. We have to go."

They quickly freed Steph and Pedro and helped them to their feet.

"That wasn't very nice," Mavis hissed as she got to one knee, still holding her hip.

Steph grabbed Emm's hand and dragged her through the store at top speed. Mavis came up behind the four of them, so angrily and powerfully that she seemed to leave a wake, sucking up glass slippers and straw bales and tossing them as she swept furiously toward the front of the store.

"Get out of the store," Steph screamed. "She's stuck in here."

John's face whitened as he watched the scene. Olly's jaw dropped too, and for a moment he forgot about his legs as the Wolf-Boy, Banana-Nose, Emm and their S & M guidance counselor ran from the satanic witch. And Mavis was gaining on the four runners very quickly. John, with Olly still in his arms, backed up and yelled "hurry!"

Pedro bounded out of the store first. Steph and Emm were not far behind. They turned as they made it into the corridor. Mr. Blake's axe slid to Emm's feet. Mr. Blake, however, was in the clutches of an extremely angry, hobbling, bubbling Mavis Stiles. She pulled him back with one hand.

"Pipsqueak!" Pedro yelled. It made Emm turn in disbelief as she remembered a name from her early, early childhood, with Browning's Traveling Oddities. *Professor Pipsqueak?* She picked up the two-handed moonstone battle axe and threw it to Professor Pipsqueak.

"Go!" Mr. Blake yelled as Mavis reeled him in.

"I'll catch up with the rest of you real soon," Mavis roared.

"You leave us alone!" Emm said.

Mavis tossed the dwarf into The Alcove. "Thanks to you and your style-conscious classmates, I won't be stuck in this go-nowhere shopping mall after tomorrow. Every pretty girl deserves to go to the ball. Ha ha ha!"

"Come on!" Steph said and ran from Spindle at top speed. They all followed. As Olly handed Emm her zombie apocalypse survival backpack, she noticed what had happened to his legs – tied in knots, bloody and misshapen worse than a ragdoll's legs. Emm cupped her mouth in horror as she sprinted through the mall.

Olly noticed Emm heaving behind her hand. "I'll be okay," Olly said. *How could he possibly be okay?*

"I'm so sorry," Emm said.

"We said we're with you til the end and we meant it," John said. "Glad you didn't come out of there with a tiara on."

"Right," Emm said. How close had she come to being a zombie? And having Loyal John loyally lop her head off? "So are we running to somewhere or just from somewhere?"

"We have to get home," Steph said. "Time to get ready for prom."

Olly's ears perked up.

Emm's didn't.

43

Olly sprawled out on the Dillingers' couch with the entire contents of the freezer on his legs. He tried to remind himself of all the Cylons' names in Battlestar Galactica, or all the Pokemons in Pokemon, or every favorite song on his iPod without looking. Anything but the pain, and his technique was almost starting to work. Almost. He was sure that any hour now he would be distracted from the pain for at least two consecutive minutes. *Leg pain is easier to deal with than heart pain*, he'd think occasionally, and feel a little relieved that at least he was distracted from that.

Pedro the Wolf-Boy and Loyal John sat across from each other on the living room floor, pouring an industrial-sized tub of SPF 99 into spray bottles.

"How does this work again, exactly?" John said as he squirted the sunblock all over the place.

"It just does," Pedro said, his fur crinkling as he lost his patience. "Mavis is a sun worshipper. Block the sun, block the power. Okay?"

"But wouldn't she just get pale?"

"Aie." Pedro smacked his forehead. "There's more to it than that, okay? Whatever wishes the star is granting,

Mavis wants to be the Queen when the changes come. She wants to take the star power and rule with it."

"If she loves the sun so much, she's gonna get skin cancer."

"Humans get skin cancer," Pedro the Wolf-Boy said and kept filling spray bottles in silence.

Steph entered from the kitchen. "Found it." She walked up to John. "Mavis probably sent out an APB to the frog princes, so anything fairy tale is going to set them off. You'll need to cover Mr. Hand, there."

John looked down at his metal hand. It didn't feel enchanted or magical or different. It just felt like his hand. He had forgotten that someone might see it as being weird.

"Here," Steph said. "The perfect disguise." She handed John the perfect disguise.

"Great," he said. It was a single, white, sequined glove. Pedro looked over from the sunscreen-pouring and smirked. Olly looked over and grinned through his grimace. He was just about to lay into John with an MJ joke when an angel in violet caught his eye.

Everyone forgot about what they were doing and what they were thinking when Emm walked into the room, wearing her disguise for their infiltration of the prom. Her disguise was far more perfect than John's. Emm was a vision in her modern, shoulderless prom dress, a deep violet with uneven hem at the bottom and empire waist. It was simple and elegant, with lacey touches making subtle accents in spots. The shoes perfectly matched. The violet was a perfect complement to Emm's opal heart-shaped necklace, which sat exposed against her sternum. Emm now knew the jewel to be moonstone, a jewel which could hurt Mavis and fight sun magic, and Emm wore it proudly. She wore the most makeup she had ever worn, even more than when she had performed as a Devastating Dillinger of Doom. Her lips were redder than ever and her eye shadow was the perfect shade of violet to match her ensemble.

"How do I look?" Emm asked sheepishly.

"Wait," John said with a suspicious look. "How much do you care about how you look?"

"Well, wearing purple makes me want to spray you all with vomit, so... I guess I must still be me."

"You look beautiful, babe," Steph said, and gave Emm a kiss on the forehead. "More importantly, how do you feel?"

"Like I want to stomp some zombie ass," Emm said. She walked over, quite formally, to Olly's couch and knelt down beside him. Olly's heart pounded as she got closer and closer. Emm looked down at his legs.

"Does it hurt?"

"Only everywhere, all the time." Olly said. They shared an awkward look. Olly would have said something snarky and possibly even mean, but he was lost in Emm's eyes.

"Olly?"

"Yeah?"

"Will you go to the prom with me? As my date?"

Olly reached for his iron cage, afraid that it may not be enough to protect his heart. "Are you serious?" Then Olly thought about his legs. "Don't do it out of pity..."

"The only thing I pity are the zombies who get in our way."

"Please, Emm. Don't make the cage any tighter. From the minute I saw you, I knew you were the one for me. I knew it." Olly was careful, almost letting each word go one at a time to make sure the word was safe to utter. "I just know in my heart that I'm supposed to be with you. But even though my heart knows it, I'm wrong."

Emm didn't shy away from Olly, even though his cage might just squeeze his heart like a balloon animal. She reached for Olly's hand. "I can't promise it won't hurt, Olly. I can't promise you're wrong, either."

Olly nodded, grudgingly. Then he looked over Emm's shoulder at Steph, who wheeled in a dusty, black leather wheelchair. Steph wiped the seat off with her hand. As Emm turned to see what Olly was looking at, her mind went back to that day in the desert, once again, when her dad slipped out of the black leather wheelchair into the sand, murdered by the sun. Tonight, Olly would use the wheelchair because the sun and its worshipper had taken Olly's legs. Emm wondered how her dad had lost his ability to walk. *Maybe I could ask him - if I ever get back to the mirror room.*

"We're going to encounter a lot of innocent Norms tonight," Steph said to the team. "The rules of engagement are simple. Self-defense only for zombies. Take the tiaras off of them if you can. Princes, you can feel free to slice and dice to your hearts' content."

"We are making a major contribution to the ASPCA after this," Emm said, thinking of the innocent froggies.

"Once her little army gathers, Mavis will have enough power in one place to make an appearance outside of Spindle, but she'll be weak enough to get got. Once they all try to summon her, we strike."

"You talk like you know this is going to happen," John said.

"It's not our first rodeo," Pedro said. "Usually they don't get this far, though."

Steph nodded. "We're getting weaker and the sun is

getting stronger. Times are changing." Steph thought of Professor Pipsqueak and hoped his end was merciful.

"Well then," Emm said with a look over at Olly. "Time to fut shick up."

44

On the way to Jacob Williams High School, Pedro whispered something in Steph's ear and Steph told John to pull over.

"Pedro wants me to give you the oath. It's kind of lame, doesn't mean anything..." Pedro nudged Steph.

"Is it a blood oath? I'm in," Olly said.

Pedro took over. "No matter where we are, we Oddities have made a vow to fight the fairy tale whenever and wherever we must. And now you join us, and so you should take the oath, si?"

"I'm ready," Emm said. She held up her right hand. Olly and John did the same. Pedro recited the oath and they followed along, line by line:

"When you wish upon a star
You show the cosmos who you are
The cosmos shows it back to you
Who you are is what you do.

We don't fit into the mold
And yet our stories must be told

Until there is but one tale left
An Oddity fights unto the death."

John started the car up as soon as it was done. Not a word was uttered the rest of the way to the prom, but Emm let herself smile, furtively, but proudly.

"Thriller Prom! Tonight!" The banner over the front entrance of Jacob Williams High School read, as the Oddities entered the zombie princess apocalypse.

Princes and tiara-wearing zombies walked into the school, arm in arm. Some had adult chaperones still; others had blood stains on their dresses. No one batted an eyelash. The Oddities each wore disguises: John and his sequined glove, Emm in her exquisite gown, Olly and Steph in tattered clothes they had snipped with a pair of scissors and rubbed in the dirt in the back yard. Pedro the Wolf-Boy went as himself, but sporting a red and black leather jacket. They each had a backpack filled with zombie survival supplies. The weight of Emm's backpack was starting to make her neck sore.

An adult chaperone walked up to Pedro and looked him up and down. "Incredible costume," the chaperone said. Pedro snarled a wolfen snarl, spraying a couple of globlets of slobber on the chaperone. "Ha ha! Very authentic!" the chaperone said and patted Pedro on the back. Pushing through the throng in the hallway, the Oddities reached the gymnasium without incident. It surprised Emm that no one was beaten, eaten, attacked or zombified. *Maybe they're waiting for something,* she thought. She reached back to her backpack and made sure the handle of her first hatchet was handy.

The gymnasium was dark, save for the scattershot

lights of three disco balls that spun lazily around. Printouts of Michael Jackson in his various incarnations, Vincent Price, Paul McCartney and the sidewalk that lights up from the *Billie Jean* video all decorated the walls. The DJ played non-stop MJ songs, starting with the early catalogue. Emm liked her music, but she had never heard any track from *Off The Wall* before. Pedro told her she was in for a treat. And that was the sum total of the Oddities' conversation as they sat on a bench, against the wall, staring out at the zombie princesses and their princes having fun on the dance floor. Mostly it was the princes who danced. About two hundred princes, Emm figured. She absently tapped her toes a bit, in time to the funk.

Emm's butt was getting sore from sitting when she asked Steph, "when does the fun start?"

"This is as fun as these things get," Steph said. "Kinda lame, huh?" It occurred to Emm that maybe Steph was as nerdy as Emm was. That had never occurred to Emm before.

"No, I mean the summony thingamadoodie that we came here to stop."

"Oh," Steph said. "When that starts, it will be obvious. There would be less milling around and more of a clustering."

"Uh-oh," John said and pointed to the dance floor. A zombie and her prince stood together, the prince holding the girl's shoulders. The girl nibbled on a bloody, beating human heart as the prince stroked her hair. A chaperone lay their feet with a fist-sized hole in his chest. Emm reached for her hatchet. "Let's go," Olly said. But Pedro held them both back.

"We can't let them do this," Olly said.

"We have to."

"Pedro's right. If we blow our cover we blow our shot. And if we let this get outside the gym, it could be the end of days."

"An apocalypse," Olly said to himself as it dawned on him that his powerpoint presentation had come true.

Emm slumped back down onto the bench and knocked her knees together. "God, this is awful," she said as the zombie princess continued to eat her parent/guardian's heart. Ironically, the macabre prelude to Thriller's title track came on over the speakers.

John rose solemnly to his feet, unable to tolerate it any longer.

"I know what I'm going to do before the apocalypse hits," John announced. "I wasn't like you guys. These dances? My friends were the ones who these dances were made to impress. We danced at these dances. I never played the wall and I'm not starting now." And with that John headed for the dance floor.

"Sit down!" Steph ordered and grabbed John's arm. When he turned to face her, his eyes steamed with tears that had been left to boil.

"I will not sit down!" John said. "I been practicing my moves for two weeks. This one... this one's for Jessica." Steph relaxed her grip. They let him go.

John dutifully walked to the center of the dance floor, trying to ignore the frog princes who eyed him suspiciously and the zombie princesses who gawked at him – maybe even coveted him. One reached for him, but was held back by her prince. At this moment, John didn't care about any of that. This moment was all about Jessica. He was going to let it all out on the dance floor, which was a major change in expressiveness from his usual step-ball-change jock dance.

He waited for his cue...

... and shot his hip out to the side.

As he went through the kicks, the moonwalk, the zombie dance and the werewolf, a circle began to form around John. He was hypnotizing them with his dancing, he thought to himself. A tear leaked from his eye as he danced. Even the DJ clapped to cheer him on. It all was so fitting. And once he was done, John thought, he would save as many as he could and then destroy every Prince Charming he could see; crush them with his bare hands; and then he would clobber Mavis for doing this to Jessica. Then the final note struck and John shot his sequin-gloved hand into the air.

Silence. The Oddities clapped from their bench on the other side of the gym. Every other being stared at John with some kind of bloodthirsty curiosity. Panting and puffing, John lowered his hand as he looked at the cocked heads and strange stares he was getting. The dance was over... now what? Then the answer came to John as his metal hand came down to his face, each metal finger reflecting the disco light prismatically. The glove was gone.

"Intruder!" a Prince Charming bellowed, pointing his dagger at John. All the zombies growled in unison and the circle tightened.

Steph facepalmed.

"He's bad, they know it," Olly said. Emm looked over at him, disgusted.

45

Pedro the Wolf-Boy launched himself from the bench. Emm pulled the first hatchet out of her pack and ran with Steph to the dance floor.

Olly tried to wheel himself, but it was tougher than he thought it would be. They left him in the dark.

All around the gym, the disco lights flashed on scenes of horror. Prince Charmings plunged their daggers into innocent chaperones and teachers. Some Prince Charming were already feeding hearts to their princesses. Three zombie princesses with the thirst for blood began to eat Mr. Hinkley. "Not cool, girls," he warned them, before another princess put her fist clean through him, entering through his back and emerging through his front to show him his heart. "Not cool" was all he could say as his blood stopped pumping.

John spun round and round as the circle closed in, not sure how to start his attack. "Form ranks!" A Prince Charming ordered, and John realized there were too many to fend off.

Pedro leaped in the air, higher than perhaps any other human being could leap, for Pedro had trained in acrobatics during the carny years, and was naturally quite agile and strong, more cat-like than dog-like, but nonetheless, Pedro was only human. He couldn't make it over all the princesses and princes who stood between him and John, and Pedro turned his high-flying leap into a barrel-roll, knocking tiaras off of several heads as he fell at John's feet.

The princesses screamed blood-curdling screams when the tiaras came off and each one, without exception, reached desperately for their tiaras and put them back on.

The Prince Charmings formed ranks, turning away from John and Pedro and drawing their daggers. The zombie princesses got closer and closer to John as he helped Pedro to his feet. Pedro the Wolf-Boy growled angrily at John.

"Oops," John said.

"Oops? We gonna die now and all you can come up with is oops? Dios mio."

Then all the Prince Charmings spoke in unison, as though they each had been overtaken by some kind of presence: Mavis.

"I know you're in here, Oddities. Show yourselves," they said in unison.

In silence, the disco lights continued to swirl. Nothing moved. The zombie princesses were so close to Pedro and John that they had to stand back-to-back.

Olly wheeled himself out of the darkness. "Here I am," he called. "I give up."

The princes marched toward him, daggers raised. Olly stared straight at them, making sure not to move his eyes no matter how desperately he wanted to see what would happen next. In his mind, Olly was not afraid to get skewered by an army of sword-bearing mutated frogs. In his mind, Olly was already picturing how Emm was going to kick their asses.

Emm had a stainless-steel hatchet in each hand as she ran across the gymnasium floor to the Princes' flank. She fell to her knees and slid on her violet gown. Emm threw the hatchets with her trademark precision; the precision that came from years of practice and unnatural talent – but this time, Emm wasn't aiming for *beside* the target's head.

Two hatchets, six princes. They were thrown with such perfect velocity and arc that each hatchet brained three princes in the middle row of their phalanx, and Emm had two more hatchets in her hand before her slide had come to a stop. The six princes instantly flash-banged into fremains or frijoles or frintestines, and all the zombies screamed in terror although they did not see what had happened. The other princes stopped marching and lowered their daggers as they looked at the frentrails in shock. Emm took the opportunity to launch two more daggers, killing four more.

"Now!" she shouted, and Steph sprinted through the space between the zombies and princes, carrying a fire extinguisher. Steph screamed as she sprayed, like she was firing a massive machine gun or a flamethrower, but the standard firefighting foam hit the zombies on the head and blasted their tiaras clear off. Steph looked over and saw John and Pedro the Wolf-Boy get swallowed up by the zombie mob. Pedro reached for Steph, hoping to get pulled from the bloodthirsty quicksand – Steph dove atop the zombie princesses and crowd surfed, stretching for Pedro's paw, but was unable to reach it. Then Pedro felt himself get picked up by the waist and he looked back to see who was lifting him.

"I'm taking one for the team," John said. "Don't worry about me. Just win," he told Pedro, and launched the Wolf-Boy by the waist toward Steph. Steph pulled Pedro free and they both looked back as John covered his heart with his metal hand.

The mob of zombies made a gurgling sound as they swallowed John up.

46

Olly held his parents' barbecue lighter in his hand and thought about blue angels. He had seen an internet video (or was it *Tosh.0*?) where some dude had taken a barbecue lighter and stuck it beneath his butt, then let her rip. As he held the aerosol can of hairspray out and sprayed it, Olly thought the blue flame was very pleasing to the eye. Incinerating princes? Even more satisfying. The fact that Emm pressed her back into the back of his wheelchair and threw hatchets like a ninja throws throwing stars? Well, that made this the best date ever.

Together, like a superhero team-up, they killed a dozen princes at least. It was totally unbelievably awesome, Olly thought. But eventually the frog princes' numbers grew to be too many and Emm leaped to her feet and wheeled Olly out of there. *Oh that's right,* Olly thought, *my legs don't work.* At least he was feeling no pain.

Emm tried to get them away from the wall, but there were too many princes. Emm couldn't move them any further without fighting. She spied Steph and Pedro, just past the princes, trying to knock tiaras off of the zombies' heads without killing them. It wasn't working.

The girls would just freak out and put the tiaras back on their heads. One zombie got a hold of Pedro's leg and sunk her teeth into it. Pedro couldn't shake himself free. Then Emm reached into her backpack and realized that there were no hatchets left.

"I'm out," she told Olly, who shook the aerosol can that didn't flame up anymore. "Me, too," Olly said. The tips of twenty daggers closed in on them both, inches away, and Emm realized that they were done for. *We tried our best,* Emm thought. *Sorry, Dad.*

"I have to say it to you, Emm," Olly said as the princes collectively smiled murderous smiles. Olly preferred to have his heart explode and ooze out of its cage, rather than get turned into a human game of Ker-Plunk. "Emm, I think I lo–"

47

Just like that, the lights turned on and nearly blinded them all. Olly shielded his eyes from the glare.

A song came through the speakers, but it wasn't Michael.

It was "When You Wish Upon A Star."

Emm looked over at the DJ booth, but the DJ fell to the floor, dead, as a zombie gnawed on his still-beating heart.

The princes raised their blades and turned around.

The zombies stood straight up, hands on their sides like proper princesses. Or robots. Pedro pulled his hind paw from the now-uninterested biter and rubbed it. "Kkkkkk," all the zombies said as they connected telepathically to the princes, who were connected telepathically to something much more sinister.

Steph caught a glimpse of John's limp body as the zombies left it. Bite marks covered him and blood dripped everywhere. But his metal hand still covered his heart. Steph couldn't be sure he was alive until he coughed and spit blood out of his mouth.

"It's time," Steph called to the kids as she followed Pedro over to John's aid. The princes and princesses moved in mobs to center court, away from the Oddities, and fell to their hands and knees. With the disco lights still swirling over them, and the demented stylings of Jiminy Cricket blaring through the speakers, the creatures began to claw at the parquet floor. They scraped and scratched and tore, breaking fingernails off in the process, tearing bits of wood that had been there for decades.

Emm wheeled Olly up to John, where Pedro and Steph wiped blood from John's face and got him to a sitting position. "He's alive," Steph told Emm, "but not for long."

"What do we do?" Emm said.

"We blow up the school," Pedro said.

"Yes!" Olly pumped his fist.

"No way," Emm said. "We're not killing innocent people. No way."

"The 'innocent people' you are talking about just murdered and ate the hearts of every innocent person in here," Pedro said, his voice more angry than it had ever been. "And now they open the gates of l'infierno."

Emm looked over at them. A red glow seeped through the cracks in the floorboards and the glow was getting brighter. Hotter, too. *Was it the fire of hell or the fire of the sun?* The air made visible waves, like the air on top of hot asphalt on a hot summer day. Hellfire or sun fire, either way, it was getting very hot in there. The red turned into an orange-white glow. The floor began to rumble, like a volcano was about to erupt in the middle of the Jacob Williams High School gym.

"It's our only chance, Emm," Steph yelled.

"We have no explosive," Pedro yelled.

Olly held up his barbecue lighter and Steph nodded.

"No!" Emm cried.

"We have to, Emm," Steph said as she reached for the handles of Derek's old wheelchair, to take Olly to the wall. But something made them all freeze.

All the monsters stepped away from the glowing opening in the floor. Emm wondered if it was a trick of the eye, or magic, or how there was not plumbing and concrete beneath the parquet. Whatever Emm was seeing, it was real enough, and it glowed like a pool of magma in the floor, casting cauldrons of heat into the gym. As though emerging from the sun itself, a human figure rose from the floor, glowing red. At was as if the glowing figure stood on the summit of a glowing white-hot mountain, and that mountain grew from the floor. Like embers when they feel the air of the bellows, the figure glowed pulsating white, then pulsated to orange, and red, and white again. As it rose further from the floor, the figure seemed to cool, and so did the mountain. The mountain looked like a mountain of glowing jeweled tiaras. Emm could make out the face. And the hair. And the little black number.

"Prom Queen? Me?" Mavis said as she glamorously strode down the mountain. Her cackling, maniacal laugh drowned out the music and the rumble in the floor.

"Burn it," Emm said. As soon as she said it, Mavis turned and pointed at her. Mavis's eyes glowed like they were on fire.

"Her," Mavis said and a brigade of Prince Charmings charged at Emm.

"Get me the necklace! Or at least the throat it's wrapped around!"

Emm clutched her necklace.

"Run!" Steph called and raced Olly to the wall, right

up to a banner that read "State Champions, Basketball, 2011." Emm turned and sprinted, pivoting down to pick up a couple of her hatchets from the floor.

"Finally," Olly said to himself. "This is a proper futting up of the shick." He held the bluish flame against the canvas banner, loaded with chemicals to make it red and make it shiny and make it weatherproof, and the banner engulfed instantly. He looked up at his handiwork, then looked over at Emm as she ran to the hallway from the gym. Emm looked back. They stole a split second to look at each other and smile. *Super hero action team,* Olly thought. Emm disappeared down the hallway, a hundred and fifty frog princes in murderous pursuit. *She'll outfox them,* he thought, completely oblivious to the cloud of patchouli stink that hovered around him.

Then, despite plenty of warning that Olly hadn't heeded, the zombified Lily Farquhar leaned into Olly's chest and started to gnaw.

48

Olly screamed in terror, but he didn't really feel anything. That scared him even more. He saw Lily's suburban dreadlocks bobbing and waggling beneath his chin as she devoured him, the beaded braids clanging against each other. He continued to scream, helpless. Then Lily pulled her head away and bared her teeth like a rabid, feral animal, aching to finish its prey. The deep crimson of fresh blood covered her swollen lips and dripped from her chin.

Olly noticed something a little peculiar about Lily's fang-baring snarl. No fangs. Lily didn't have any teeth at all; merely bloody gums that bled all over her mouth and down her chin. All the teeth were sitting on Olly's lap, broken off as Lily attempted to eat her way through the enchanted iron cage. Lily had failed, despite her best attempts, to eat any red meat at all.

As a bloodthirsty zombie princess with twenty-two broken teeth, this did not impress Lily Farquhar. Especially since she thought herself better than a geek like Oliver Ford with every fibre of her being. She got ready to rip his throat out with her bare hands.

Pedro the Wolf-Boy thought it vulgar to use claws in

this manner, despite the fact that each of his fingernails were as sharp and strong as dew claws. Instead, he pounced behind Lily Farquhar with a length of razor-wire, wrapped it around her throat and very cleanly decapitated her.

Lily's head rolled onto Olly's lap and he screamed in shocked disgust, spasmodically sweeping with his hands until her head rolled to the floor. Olly panted as his brain ingested what had just happened. Pedro watched Lily's body collapse onto the floor.

"You could have given me a heads-up," Olly said with mock anger.

Pedro shuddered at the awful joke.

"They just fall out of me like nervous farts," Olly said.

The battle continued.

49

Emm was in full stride as she ran past the lockers, dozens of princes in pursuit. There was no point in trying to stop and fire her hatchets; there were too many to kill them all, not to mention they would catch up the second she slowed down.

She needed a place to hide. Quick.

She saw a door and went through it, slamming it shut. As she locked it, she read the backwards name on the frosted glass: "Guidance Counselor." Mr. Blake's office. The princes pounded on the door and it nearly buckled. It was just a matter of time before the princes would break through and kill her. She backed away from the door, ready to fight to her last breath. The door bounced again, nearly out of the doorframe. A crack crept up the frosted glass. Emm gripped her hatchets. Ready. *Ready to die.*

"Aren't you going to say hello?" said a voice from behind her, and Emm shrieked. Bruised and beaten, still in his S&M guidance counselor fatigues, Mr. Blake sat at his desk, moonstone axe resting on his piles of paperwork. *Professor Pipsqueak.*

"Why do they want my necklace?"

"Because it can stop Mavis." With a grunt, Mr. Blake/ Professor Pipsqueak slid the axe into his hands. "I could never talk sense into your father, but at least he was reasonable enough to put some moonstone around your neck."

A third pounding on the door. The Prince Charmings were either ramming the door in unison, or using one of the Charmings as a battering ram. Professor Pipsqueak grunted and tried to get out of the chair, onto his feet. It wasn't working.

"That's why we sent you to Spindle... a little help here?" Emm guided Professor Pipsqueak by his elbow and he got to his feet. The glass in the door lost a chunk and a frog prince hand poked through the hole and felt its way around.

"Steph didn't think you were ready, but Mavis had grown too powerful to wait. In fact, we waited too long. Be ready now." Kick after kick turned the bottom of the door into splinters. The hand reached in further and further.

"Why me?" Emm asked. "It's not like I'm Supergirl. I'm just... weird."

Professor Pipsqueak swept the papers off his desk and climbed on top, with a shove from Emm.

"Yes. Odd. This is who we are, Emm. We are Oddities. Our story is the odd one. If it wasn't for our stories, all the stories would become one story. We'd all be zombies." He rose to his feet, on top of his desk, and readied his two-handed battle axe. "Once we stop changing – growing – the universe will just feed us to ourselves. That's where you come in."

"That's where I come in."

"It's your story now, Emm. You will lead us Oddities in our final battle, to save the Normals from themselves."

"How do I do that?"

The door shattered into a million shards. The glass fell away and all the wood splintered like a car wash curtain.

"Fight."

Princes clogged the open doorway as they clamored to get through. Emm and Professor Pipsqueak took advantage. Emm slashed with her hatchets, her back against the wall adjacent to the doorway. Pipsqueak leaped with his battle-axe overhead, coming down on the lot of them.

Back in the gym, flames rose up the wall easily and quickly as Mavis strode through the carnage. Corpses and gore were spread everywhere. Pieces of fibrous ceiling material fell to the floor as the fire got nearer and nearer. Princesses, with armfuls of tiaras, made their way to the exits.

Steph, Olly and Pedro gathered around John's badly injured body. Olly reached into his backpack and wrapped his fingers around a spray bottle of SPF 99. He curled his index finger around the trigger as Mavis approached.

"You've made a mistake coming here, Mavis. You're too far from home," Steph said.

"Piffle," Mavis said. She moved her hands like a puppeteer moves them to manipulate a marionette, and John's limp body levitated ten feet into the air. Mavis let her fingers do the walking, and John's body did the moonwalk. Then she unceremoniously dropped him to the floor. "I'm tired of you freaks getting in the way of good fashion sense. Give me Emm and her necklace, or you all die. Kay?"

"The only thing you're getting is SPF 99," Olly said in

his best growly Dark Knight voice, and whipped out the spray bottle of sunscreen. He shot Mavis up and down. Steph pulled her bottle out from behind her and sprayed, getting Mavis right in the face.

Nothing happened.

"Ha! I found some sunblock... block," Mavis declared. "The answer is always a good concealer." Then she walked up to Olly and took a whiff. Steph and Pedro knew there was no way to stop her, so they waited for an opening. Mavis lifted Olly out of the wheelchair with an easy gesture and, once he got eye level, she ripped open his shirt with her bare hands. She saw the metal bars around his heart.

"I thought I smelled unrequited love. That's one of my personal favorites. You'll do."

"No!" Pedro yelled and tried to attack. Mavis merely made a flipping movement with her hand and Pedro the Wolf-Boy did a pile driver into the floor. Steph had no choice but to try something, but Mavis just lifted a single finger at her. "Ah-ah, Mrs. Dillinger. Why don't you stay here." Mavis sniffed in Steph's direction. "I sense... I sense a wish in you, too. A little more normal than you'd care to admit, I'm sure. Oooh, yum yum. That's a juicy one, Stephanie."

In an instant, the leather wheelchair sped over to Steph and hit the back of her legs, forcing her to sit down. Strips of leather pulled themselves from the back and seat, binding Steph around the waist, arms and ankles.

"We could have been such a good team," Mavis said, "the wicked stepmother and the queen of hearts! Ah, well." And Steph watched Mavis walk out of the inferno, with Olly as her puppet. Scraps of flaming ceiling fell all around them. All Steph could think about was how utterly normal she turned out to be, to have her heart's wish be that Derek Dillinger had never sacrificed his spine to save hers

50

Professor Pipsqueak and Emm hacked and slashed at the bridgehead of princes, who clamored so competitively to get through the doorway that it was child's play to reduce them to frog guts. Green sputum and whitish intestines covered the walls and floors and their clothes and faces. Pipsqueak, also known as Mr. Blake, hadn't taken a single hit. Emm had a thin scratch on her cheek, from where the very tip of a dagger blade had made its way through the fracas and touched her flesh. The Prince Charming who had scratched her smiled with pride when he realized what he had done. Made it pretty easy for Emm to chop him up. Now, only a dozen princes remained and the battle looked to be nearly won. Emm felt like she was in the final mile of the Boston Marathon.

"This is some pretty serious cardio," Emm said as she backed away a little, trying to catch her breath.

"You're quite good at close range," Pipsqueak said. "Watch out – "

Too late. A Prince cut Emm's chest with the tip of his blade; as the blade lifted, it caught Emm's necklace. The Prince parked the dagger and was just about to lurch forward and skewer Emm in the hollow of the throat, but Pipsqueak leaped at his back and cleaved him.

"If Mavis gets hold of that necklace, we can't stop her," he told Emm as he performed a no-look parry and held off a lunging Prince Charming.

"What does she want?"

"She got what she wants. She's a sun worshipper and she's found the gateway to unimaginable power. The unseen power of the universe itself."

"Oh, sure. Unseen power of the universe. Of course."

"It has a name, but no one dares speak it. Call it The Thing That Makes It So."

"So we kill Mavis and win, right? How do we kill her?"

"You contain her. You can't kill her. Universe won't allow it."

"Like Lucky Miller."

Pipsqueak shot Emm a look of surprise and nearly got stabbed for his trouble. "You've met Lucky," he said, but he didn't sound very impressed at all. "They say Lucky plucked the hairs off the devil himself."

"The devil is real?"

"In a matter of speaking. Be wary of him. He's trying to... well... get lucky." That made Emm a little more flush than she already was. There was something that drew her to Lucky Miller. *He did seem kind of devilish...*

"I thought he was on our side."

"Lucky is not on our side. Nor is he on theirs. Lucky is on Lucky's side. Remember that," he grunted as he made his way to the final Prince Charming and reduced him to green spatter.

"We did it!" Emm said. *No more blood thirst. That ought to save a whole passel of lives.* But then Emm saw Olly float into view like a marionette, his twisted legs dangling three feet from the floor. "Olly?"

The black Louboutins of Mavis Stiles clip-clopped behind Olly, using him as a shield. Pipsqueak and Emm gave each other a look and readied their weapons.

"Yoo-hoo," Mavis said. "I've got a whopper of a limited-time offer for you." Emm didn't have a shot at Mavis. She would have hit Olly no matter what she tried. Not to mention Mavis's power might have grown strong enough to toss her throwing hatchets aside, or even back at Emm. "Give me the necklace and I spare this boy's life. You know, this one." She jiggled Olly a little bit as though Emm and the Oddities didn't know which boy she was referring to. "The one who loves you, but who you don't love back. Such a tragic tale."

"We're going to finish this right here, Mavis," Pipsqueak said.

"Wait –" Emm recalled what Mr. Blake had just said to her. Mavis could not be killed. Mavis needed to be contained. She didn't see any way that could happen without Mavis having ample opportunity to kill Olly.

"Yes," Mavis said through a grin and a dark look. "Do think about it. But act now, because this offer won't be available for long."

Emm took hold of her necklace and thought back to the illusion her dad did for her, making it disappear and reappear, just seconds before he disappeared from this world. Emm got a peek at Mavis, who still casually used Olly as a shield. She seemed to be inspecting her fingernails.

"As we kibbutz," Mavis said, blowing on her cuticles,

"my little army of zombie princesses are out on the town, passing tiaras to every Snow White, Cinderella, Sleeping Beauty, Liberace, and whatever other princess there may be in this town. By dawn, my power will be so great I'll buy out Forever 21. So you see, I really can't be stopped. You might as well spare your pretzel-legged friend here from a slow death."

Professor Pipsqueak shook his head vehemently at Emm. She still held on to the heart shaped locket of moonstone.

Then Olly stirred, coming to a very low level of consciousness. "Please..." Olly rasped, "the necklace." He held out his trembling hand.

He's done all he can. And what have I done for him? Emm pulled on her locket.

"No!" Pipsqueak bellowed. "We can fight her. We can stop them."

"Aw, isn't the heart a terrible thing?" Mavis said as she stepped out from behind Olly.

"Please..." Olly rasped again.

Emm tugged at the locket so hard that the clasp tore apart. Pipsqueak's jaw dropped and shoulders slumped. Mavis's smile exposed every perfectly-whitened tooth.

Emm placed the necklace into Olly's outstretched hand and closed his fingers around it. He looked into her eyes and she looked into his. They shared a smile of consolation. Of surrender. "I'm sorry," Olly whispered.

And then he smashed the necklace onto Mavis's forehead. The moonstone flashed a milky-white light and Mavis fell back, tortured by the necklace. Her arms flailed as she threw Olly down and clutched her head. Then she kicked Olly in the head with her designer heels. Olly's head snapped back and Emm heard a pop like breaking of a tree branch. It was the snapping of Olly's spine.

Professor Pipsqueak leaped through the air with his two-handed moonstone battle axe, this time with blade forward, and dug into Mavis's lungs. The axe lay buried there, and Mavis stared at it in disbelief. Then Pipsqueak stomped on the moonstones with his boot and buried them into Mavis.

She looked up at the little man with wide eyes. Then she became burning embers again, red, orange, pulsating white, and then grey. She turned to ash and left nothing but a heap of dust so fine and light, the school's air conditioning system blew it in circles.

Mavis had been destroyed.

The fire alarms sounded. The sprinklers turned on and rained down on Emm. But she didn't notice.

Olly's body couldn't take any more. He was gone.

51

"Olly," Emm cried over and over. She cradled him in her lap. His eyes were still open, but perfectly still. Emm put her ear against his mouth, desperately wishing for breath to come and warm her ear. It never came. She leaned against his chest, against his caged heart, and wished for a heartbeat, but she did not hear one.

Olly was dead.

"I'm sorry, child." Professor Pipsqueak rested a hand on Emm's shoulder as she melted into tears.

"You should have never been my friend," she said. "I did this to you."

This time, it was no joke. I killed Olly. Maybe I killed Dad, too. All of this is my fault.

She looked into Olly's dead eyes and an idea swam into her mind. A strange idea. A wonderful idea.

If I am some kind of superheroic leader, and so was my Dad, and the sun grants wishes, then I am going to make my wish come true. If magic is alive in us, then dammit, I am going to use it. Dad was a magician. So am I.

Emm wiped her tears away and got determined. She leaned in, closer and closer, her lips trembling, for this was the first kiss she had ever given a boy, and her blood-red lips quivered as they offered Olly's cadaver the sweetest, gentlest kiss she could offer. And on her lips was a wish. A wish for Olly to come back to her.

If Professor Pipsqueak had brought a magnifying glass or the monocle he had used in his sideshow act, he would have been able to observe the microscopic space between Emm's mouth and Olly's. Then he would have seen the spectrum-colored mist that travelled from Emm's breath to Olly's, for Derek Dillinger had been wrong. Magic is visible. And Emm used the visible magic she did not know she could control, and she made her heart's true selfless wish come true. It wasn't necessarily romantic love – the kind they talk about in Disneyfied fairy tales – but it was a kind of caring love that she had in her heart. And it worked.

The little freak came back to life.

Olly blinked and then blinked faster. Emm couldn't believe it. Neither could Professor Pipsqueak, who kneeled and seemed to genuflect, like he had just witnessed a miracle. *You can't bring back the dead*, he thought to himself.

Olly looked up into Emm's eyes, which now flooded with tears of joy. "That... was magical," Olly said and they shared a tiny, beautiful laugh.

Emm slipped her arms around him and they embraced, and as her chest pressed up against his, the magical metal cage around his heart loosened so much that his heart could swell up.

It pumped magnificently.

52

It was at this point that Emm realized she was soaking wet, and that it was because of the sprinkler system, and the sprinkler was triggered by the fire alarm, and the fire alarm was triggered by a fire, which was what Olly had started in the gymnasium in order to destroy the school they were still inside.

She tried to scoop Olly up, but she wasn't strong enough. "Come on," the Professor said, "up we get," and dragged Olly by the arms, up and over his back. Olly's twisted-up legs dragged on the floor as they made their way down the hall. Emm picked up the two handed battle axe for Professor Pipsqueak. She admired its heft.

Straggling zombies continued to find their way out of the school, drenched and carrying as many tiaras as they could. Smoke billowed into the hallway from the gym.

"Now that they won't kill anybody, we should just leave them be," Emm said.

"Not that simple," said the Professor. "All it takes is one bloodthirsty princess to show the rest."

"Mavis?" Olly asked.

"Dead."

"Not dead," Professor Pipsqueak corrected Emm. "Just delayed."

A zombie princess growled and attacked Pipsqueak from behind – perfect opportunity to try the battle axe. Emm pulled up with both hands, raised the thing over her head – *man this is heavy!* – and struck, splitting the zombie's head in two from top to bottom, right down the middle. It was very different from a throwing hatchet, she thought. But it worked. The diminutive duo turned to admire Emm admiring her own handiwork. "Come on," she said, but as she said it, two more zombies descended upon her.

Emm drop-kicked zombie princess A in the empire waist, cleaved zombie princess B with a baton-like twirl of the battle axe, then tried a throw of the axe. She spun, letting go of the massive thing, and fell to a crouch as she decapitated zombie princess A. She caught her breath as zombie princess B's torso went limp and came down to the floor. As Emm got up, she saw movement in the corner of her eye. It was the zombie from before with her head split down the middle. She wasn't dead. Instead, she was taking a bite out of Olly's shoulder. Instinctively, Emm reached back, pulled a hatchet out of her backpack and tossed it perfectly.

Nope, stickin with the hatchets.

Olly brushed the zombie head off of his shoulder and glowered at Emm. "*Separate* the head from the body next time."

"Sor-ry," she smiled, relieved that Olly seemed like himself again.

They burst through the front doors and scanned the school grounds. A few zombies could be seen in the distance, but none appeared to threaten them. Steph, Pedro and John were nowhere to be seen. Emm handed the Professor his battle axe. "They're not out here. We have to go back inside."

Professor Pipsqueak slid Olly off of his back and rubbed his kidneys. "Neither of us are very mobile," Professor Pipsqueak said. "I'm useless to you with Oliver on my back."

"I have to go in," Emm said. The boys nodded.

She could hear "When You Wish Upon A Star" long before she got inside the gym. The song sounded mangled now, the speakers melting as they broiled in the flames. The sprinklers had no chance. Emm couldn't see anything in the smoke. "Steph?" She called out. "Mom?"

"Here!" Came a voice close to the volcanic gash at center court. It made the smoke red and soon, Emm could make out a blob-shaped silhouette in the smoke – the wheelchair. And Steph attached to it. Pedro was gnawing at the leather straps. John was awakening now, rubbing his head and trying to stand up. He looked wobbly.

"Got it!" Pedro yelled as the strap broke. Steph slid her legs out.

"We have to get out of here!" Emm yelled at them. The roar of the inferno was almost louder than Emm's loudest voice.

"Can you walk?" Steph yelled at John.

But John didn't say a word. Or even offer a facial expression in response. He just rose all the way up to his feet. From the smoke and redness of the gymnasium inferno, a flaming zombie ran at the Oddities, berserk and burning. A scream filled her throat. *She was a girl once*, Emm thought. *A girl like me. Except normal. With normal wishes and dreams. All she wanted to be was a princess.* And now John caught the blazing berserker with his metal hand as she leaped, trying to kill all of them. She hung there for a moment, burning, screaming, growling, flailing, suspended by Loyal John's iron hand.

Without so much as a grimace, Loyal John took his metal hand and pulled, with all his might. Without so much as a grimace, Loyal John ripped the zombie's head from her body. He did it matter-of-factly. He did it without talking or feeling. He just did it.

Emm wheeled the wheelchair as they escaped the burning gym, just as half the roof finally collapsed onto the floor.

The blaze lit up the night sky as the Oddities gathered in the schoolyard. They could hear the sirens of police cars and fire engines, but none came to Jacob Williams High School. The streets around the school looked like Halloween night, but the trick-or-treaters were collecting princesses and human hearts. And they roamed, their numbers legion now, crisscrossing the streets and going from home to home. The Oddities looked on in disgust.

"We can't kill them all even if we wanted to," Emm said.

"But didn't we kill Mavis?" Olly said as he re-set himself in the wheelchair. "Why didn't all the bad just go poof?"

"We have to get closer to the source and unplug Mavis from it," Steph said.

Emm figured it out. "Spindle."

53

They piled into Loyal John's car. John still hadn't said a word, but he drove, with Steph and Emm piled into the front seat; Professor Pipsqueak, Pedro the Wolf-Boy, and Olly crammed together in the back so that there was room for Olly's torn-up wheelchair and all the zombie princess apocalypse survival kits, which had proven to be somewhat handy.

The drive from school to the mall was as macabre as the school dance. Streetlights toppled over, smashed on top of vehicles whose drivers had been murdered. Zombies wandered everywhere, some still with spare tiaras to place on the heads of those who wished the wrong wish. *Life as we know it is over,* Emm thought. *Zombie Princess Apocalypse.* Although 'zombie' was really just shorthand for mindless subhuman. It's not like they were already dead, and it wasn't like they wanted to eat brains. No, no, these girls just wanted to be pretty, and then they wanted to eat your heart out. *Maybe that's exactly life as we know it.*

The glow of house fires could be seen all over the horizon, like torches in a dark cave. They illuminated the night sky. Sirens continued to wail, but as the Oddities drove, they didn't see a single other car in motion. Others must have taken to hiding by now. Maybe soon the army would come and wipe Modesta right off the map.

"Emm?" Olly tapped on her shoulder. She turned, happy for the distraction. "Something important," Olly said. "We need superhero names. If we're going to be a zombie slayer super-team, with Mr. Blake as Professor Pipsqueak, and Pedro the Wolf-Boy – and hey by the way, why are you not a wolf *man*?" Pedro shrugged. "Pedro the Wolf-Boy... Loyal John... we should all get cool names."

"Okay, Olly. I'll play along. So who am I, and don't say Emily the Strange."

Olly considered it very seriously. Professor Pipsqueak looked away, wanting nothing to do with this conversation.

"You and your stepmother are the Devastating Dillingers of Doom," Pedro said. "Three D."

"That's lame," Steph interjected. "I don't need a name. I don't have anything that's super about me anyway, so..."

"How about Wicked Stepmother?" Emm suggested. "Except wicked like in the Boston sense of the word." Steph rolled the words around in her head and smiled.

"Divine Miss Emm? Emmazing Lass? Emminemm? Emmenthal?"

"Let's do you, Olly."

Olly pursed his lips. "Well, Iron Man is taken... you know what? I'm going to take ownership of the pejorative name the bastards at school called me because I was in the lowest percentile for height."

"Take ownership. Great idea. Wait, what did they call you?"

"Sperm. Wait! Sperminator! Call me The

Sperminator."

"Umm, no," Emm said. "Let's just stick with Emm and Olly."

They car wheeled up to the Modesta Shopping Center slowly. The shopping mall doors were smashed and all the power was off. They got themselves organized, strapped Olly into the wheelchair, readied their weapons and went inside.

Emergency lights flickered as Emm poked her head through the broken door. She twisted a bit and unlocked the door so Olly could be pushed through. John pointed at TGI Friday's. Two black-haired zombie princesses with Hello Kitty purses dined on the heart of the TGI Friday's hostess.

"I don't think that's on the menu," Olly said.

Pipsqueak shushed him. "Be quiet," he hissed.

"And alert," Pedro said. They crept through the mall, trying not to attract attention to themselves. Emm was nervous but determined as she led them through. *Time to stop this insanity.*

Olly gripped the hammer and metal spike as he looked to the stern and aft of his wheelchair. Then, without warning, or any reason he could see, the wheelchair stopped. Olly looked left and right, behind him, and then finally downward – and noticed the corpse that his wheels had become stuck on. He turned to tell Pedro, who was pushing his chair.

"Speed bump," Olly said with a nervous grin.

"Shhh," Pedro began, but it became "uuunhggggh" as a zombie sunk her teeth into Pedro's side. He sidestepped to try and get her off of him, and Olly got a good look from his wheelchair: this zombie looked to be about ninety years old with blue hair. Not the target demographic. Mavis must have been getting stronger. Pedro struggled to get the zombie off of him, and as he pushed her away, Olly saw Steph, behind

Pedro, covered in four zombies. "Guys," Olly called, as each zombie chewed on one of Steph's limbs. A zombie hand with a tiara in it reached up, up to place it on Steph's head.

"Steph!" Emm yelled and ran to the back of the line. Pedro finally put down the elderly zombie with his razor wire, but was too tired to come to Steph's aid. John and Pipsqueak rushed over, but they were all too late. The tiara was on Steph's head.

Emm only got as far as Olly's wheelchair before Steph became a zombie. Emm froze in terror as she watched Steph twitch. Her eyes became vacant. Her lip convulsed and let some drool leak from her mouth.

Pipsqueak and John kept fighting. John punched one in the face while Pipsqueak hacked another in two and dealt it a decapitating death blow as it writhed on the floor.

Then another zombie came, from out of nowhere, and attacked Olly, grabbing his hammer-wielding wrist. This zombie was male. A middle-aged male. In a business suit.

Loyal John and Professor Pipsqueak finished off the fourth and final zombie. They looked at each other with a smile of congratulations on some solid teamwork. Then they looked over at Steph. She growled in reply.

"Uh oh," John said.

The Professor held up his axe. "Get the tiara off," he told John.

Emm climbed onto the male zombie's back and pulled at him, moving enough to avoid getting a bite while freeing Olly from the zombie's grip. Olly swung the hammer and nailed the zombie in the side of the head. As he fell, unconscious, face-first, Emm dug a knee into his back.

"Decapitate, please," Olly said pleasantly.

Emm pulled a hatchet out of her backpack and raised it over the man's head. But then she took a breath. *One more chance.* She flicked the tiara off of his head and turned back to see if Steph was okay.

She wasn't. John had lifted her with his metal hand and was trying to delicately remove the tiara with his other hand. Zombie Steph dug her teeth into John's wrist. John cried out and reactively swiped at Steph's head and just about clubbed her, but knocked the tiara off instead. Steph returned to consciousness, her teeth still dug into John's forearm. She removed her jaws from him like a scolded dog.

"Sorry," she said to John.

Emm's male zombie princess was regaining his consciousness. Emm turned him over to look him in the eye. He blubbered, the tears making his blood-soaked face shine. "*You* want to be a princess," Emm said to him, not really believing it. But the guy nodded, despite the pain this admission seemed to cause. And then, like a lightning bolt, his arm shot out and he snatched the tiara from two feet away.

"Aw, come on," Emm said to herself. He put the tiara back on and shoved Emm off of him. She took the push and rolled backward nimbly, sprung to her feet, and beheaded him with two hatchets in a crossing motion. The head, still with tears on it, rolled to the wheel of Olly's wheelchair.

"You tried," Olly said.

"I tried."

Pedro was shaken up pretty badly by the ninety-year-old's attack on his side, so Steph had to wrap Pedro's arm around her shoulders to keep him on his feet. "Let's get upstairs," Steph said to the rest of the Oddities. But a little voice in Steph's head told her things that made her very sad. When Emm asked her if she was okay, Steph tried to stuff that sadness down deep, and Steph wondered if her eyes could mask how awful she felt and how badly she wanted to put that tiara back on. She told her stepdaughter she was fine and started to hump Pedro to the escalators.

So not fine, the sadness said. *Once you do it, you never fully undo it.*

54

Emm and Professor Pipsqueak led them up the escalator. John carried Olly up, wheelchair and all; Olly kept his hammer and spike at the ready. Steph let Pedro rest himself against the guardrail as they brought up the rear.

They're chipping away at us, Steph thought. Pedro was almost incapable of fighting at this point. John was acting like he wasn't hurt, but he surely was. They all had nicks and bites at this point. *We can't take much more of this.*

"Mr. Blake? Two o'clock," John said. Two zombies rode the escalator down, coming right for them.

"Got it," Pipsqueak said. He readied his battle axe. Emm got ready to throw, but the zombies were moving, and coming downward at an angle to boot. Emm hadn't practiced that one.

Two gunshots rang out. Big fat gunshots. The blasts hit each zombie in the chest, pushing them over the edge of the escalator and down to the main floor. *They're not dead*, Emm thought as her eyes followed them down, *but they're not our problem anymore.* When Emm's eyes looked back up, she saw Lucky Miller coming down the escalator, a smoking .44 Magnum in each hand, a smoking cigarette butt in his mouth. *Of course he smokes. He's the one guy who won't get cancer.*

"You again?" Olly said. Lucky bounded over from escalator to escalator, landed a step beneath Emm, and spit out his cigarette. Olly got ready for the heart pain to come back.

"Quite the mess you made, Oddballs," he said. He bounded up to Emm's step and nearly pressed his chest against her as she turned to watch him. Professor Pipsqueak's warning about Lucky never entered her mind. All she could think about was Lucky's breath, which smelled awful and enticing at the same time, and how she wanted him to lean forward a bit more, even closer.

Instead, Lucky shot an arm over Emm's shoulder and pistol-whipped a zombie in the face. Emm glanced up the stairs past Lucky's arm: six zombie princesses lay in wait for the Oddities at the top of the escalator. She looked back as her eyes met Lucky's. There was fire in Lucky's eyes. An ancient fire.

Lucky Miller looked softly back into Emm's eyes. "Hi, Emm."

"Hi," she said back, her cheeks flushing. All of the Oddities attacked the zombies together, with Lucky included, as they got off of the escalator steps.

"Lucky, what is it you want?" Steph barked at Lucky as they drop-kicked, punched and scrapped their way toward Spindle.

"You need my help," Lucky said.

"Debatable," Professor Pipsqueak said. Lucky tried to end the debate. Without looking, Lucky put his gun behind his back and fired, shooting a zombie princess in the face. Lucky turned, looked over at the Professor and winked.

"Oh, snap! How you like me now?" Lucky said.

Professor Pipsqueak launched himself toward Lucky, axe-first. Lucky dodged the attack, but then realized it was never meant for him. Face-shot-out princess had risen from the floor behind Lucky and would have attacked him from behind. Instead, the Professor lopped her legs off at the knees and she fell down to his height, where he could take a two-handed swing in the other direction and finish the job.

"I don't," the Professor said to Lucky. "I don't like you at all." Professor Pipsqueak and Lucky Miller found a new fight together.

A male zombie with a "Choose Life" t-shirt overpowered Pedro. John took care of him with a horse-collar tackle and twist with John's metal hand.

Two zombies hurled themselves at the group from either side of the Modesta Shopping Center corridor. Lucky stretched his arms out and fired both guns at once, dropping both zombies simultaneously.

"You need all the luck you can get right now," Lucky told Steph.

"I'd rather be good than lucky," Steph said as she kicked the last zombie in the breadbasket and thrusted the zombie over to Professor Pipsqueak, who used the zombie's own momentum to force her neck onto his blade. The pack of zombies were defeated. Nothing stood between them and Spindle.

Lucky slid his .44 Magnums into his waistband. "Right now, we need to be both." He coolly pulled out his pack of Lucky Strikes, lit one, and gestured to Spindle's storefront, which was closed up.

Behind the security glass, there were so many zombies it looked like a fish tank that was all fish and no water.

Blood smears painted the glass as the zombies thrashed about and writhed in a mass, young zombie princesses and old zombie princesses, female zombie princesses and male zombie princesses, all moving and throbbing like a tumor inside the store.

"What do we do?" Emm asked Steph.

Steph looked out at the zombie mob with squinted eyes. She was so tired. Her body told her to give up. Her mind told her to join the mob.

"We have to get past them," Steph said.

"I don't think I can do it," Pedro the Wolf-Boy said. Steph knew he couldn't. He couldn't even stand up straight. John continued to bleed from a dozen places, but didn't say a word. The battle had left Olly handicapped, and he wasn't even strong enough to move his own wheelchair. And the last thing Steph wanted to do was put Emm in danger, but Steph remembered certain vows she had made to Emm's parents. And Steph would rather die than break those vows.

"We have to try, Pedro," Steph said.

At which point the security glass, without a hint of warning, gave way, and a thousand bloodthirsty zombies spilled out in front of them.

55

The Oddities formed ranks as the zombies trampled other zombies underfoot in their mad assault on the fresh meat. In about ten seconds, the zombies would be upon them. Emm tapped her backpack and made herself ready.

"I really wish I could run away right now," Olly said.

"Here," Lucky tossed him two cans of Spindle Aerosol Hair Helmet Spray.

Olly dug around in his backpack for his barbecue lighter. Steph saw something, reached into Olly's pack, and withdrew an extra-large pair of hedge clippers.

"Kill as few as you can," Steph told the team. The Oddities each shot her a look and Steph realized that her extra-large hedge clippers didn't exactly scream "show mercy."

"Just get us to the change room," she told Lucky Miller.

"As you wish, milady," Lucky said.

He fired both guns and hit two zombies. Emm decapitated four with two solid throws of the hatchet, then slid along the floor on her dress and picked up the hatchets to strike again. Pedro found the strength to pounce, and he climbed atop a male zombie and began to thrash. John pounded his way through them, nearly oblivious to bites and scratches as he used his fist like a sledgehammer. Professor Pipsqueak used his tried-and-true – take them down at the knees, bring them down to his level, then off with their heads.

"Why the change room?" Emm asked Steph.

Steph stabbed one in the gut, then withdrew the hedge clippers and snipped at the zombie's throat. "If we destroy the change room --"

"... we cut the cord," Professor Pipsqueak finished her sentence.

Olly fired up his blue angels with the new aerosol cans. "What, is it like some portal to a nether-dimension or something?"

"It's a short-cut to the Thing That Makes It So," Steph said.

The Oddities pushed against the tide of zombies, hacking and slashing a path toward the store. Pedro stayed above them, leaping from head to head and knocking tiaras off. John pummeled zombies as he brought up the rear, protecting Olly as he had vowed to do. Lucky pressed both barrels into the stomach of a zombie and fired, then took Emm's hand and pulled her forward. Steph and the Professor battled back-to-back.

"What is it making so? The Thing That Makes It So?" Emm asked. "Is it the global cooling time. An ice age?"

"You could say that," Professor Pipsqueak said. "An ice age of the heart."

"Let me see if I got all this straight for my blog," Olly said as flames streamed from his wheelchair. "You wish on a star. If the wish is strong enough, like if enough people share the wish, the stars make it come true. Except be careful what you wish for, because the universe just basically does what it pleases."

"Wrong," Steph said. "It's not us versus universe. We are the universe. It's us versus us."

"Gee, Mrs. Dillinger, that's pretty depressing."

"There's a place," the Professor said, "where The Thing That Makes It So lives. It is a hot place. A fiery place. Fires create as much as they destroy when they burn. And the Thing That Makes It So," – he paused to decapitate a zombie – "It uses the fire to create the universe we want. Unfortunately, we don't all want the same thing."

"Zombies are big these days. Fairy tales are big these days. Makes sense." Olly set two zombies' hair on fire.

"So you guys want *me* to fight the whole will of the universe," Emm said, "and save us all from an ice age that I don't even get. Sounds real fair."

Lucky blasted his way to what used to be the window display area of Spindle. The throng showed no signs of abating; hundreds of people with a wish to be some part of a fairy tale all descended upon them, looking to devour them, possibly just because they didn't share the same wish.

John gave Olly another shove with his foot and then fought with his fists. With every punch, he thought of Jessica. Every single punch. He wished he could stop hurting people, but Loyal John had made a vow to protect Olly, and then Emm, and they both needed his protection right now.

Steph was merciless as she hedge-clipped the mob of men and women who threatened them. As tiaras fell and got picked back up, the impulse to grab the tiara and put it on her own head nearly overwhelmed Steph. But she kept going back to her vow. *Get her ready,* she had promised. *Take care of Derek and get her ready to lead the Oddities.*

"But I'm normal," she had told them, fifteen years ago.

"No one is normal," Daphne Dillinger told Steph. "You are as special as anyone on this Earth. Now promise me." And so Steph had promised. Now she intended to deliver.

"Cans of whoop ass, please," Steph yelled to Olly. Olly nodded. He pulled two beer cans out of his backpack – with masking tape labels that read "whoop ass" – shook them up, then tossed them into the crowd. Each one exploded on impact, obliterating a dozen zombies each.

"Where did you learn that?" John said.

"Anarchist's Cookbook," the Sperminator said as he puffed his chest out.

The explosions were enough to get them to the back of the store. Emm caught a glimpse of the entrance to The Alcove, still a pile of rubble to either side of the wall, but the curtain was closed.

"Look," Emm pointed, "the zombies won't cross the rope." The red velvet rope seemed to keep them at bay. The Oddities rushed for it and, sure enough, the zombies roared and gnashed their teeth, but did not cross.

Emm opened the giant red velvet curtain and peered inside, into The Alcove. She saw a narrow room with grey stones and mildew and long candles in a row. At the back of The Alcove, sipping her tea, was Mavis Stiles. She luxuriated in a Queen Victoria highback chair.

"Come, come, all of you," Mavis said, as though they were old friends. As though they hadn't just destroyed her.

Emm didn't know what to do, but Steph urged her to go in and the rest of the Oddities followed.

56

Mavis sipped her tea patiently, casually bobbing a leg and bouncing the red sole of her unscuffed Louboutins. She didn't have a scratch on her face. As Lucky Miller came through the curtain, Mavis stopped.

"Oh, hello, Lucky," she said.

"Mavis."

"Lucky, shouldn't you be leaving now?"

A strange, fearful expression came over Lucky's face. "I... *should* be leaving now," he droned. The muscles in Lucky's neck seemed to tense up. A little blood threatened to leak out of his nostril.

"That's a good little fairy tale," Mavis said. But Lucky did not leave. Emm could tell that Lucky was struggling against some kind of influence, and that made her proud.

"Give up, Mavis," Emm said. "We will never stop."

"Oh really?" Mavis stood up and tossed her teacup behind her. "Feeling infinite, are we? Against the infinite power of infinity itself? Seems a little, well, fantastical, doesn't it?"

Professor Pipsqueak jumped in front of Emm and gave Mavis his best threatening look. "Come at me, Mavis."

"Like I said, Lucky needs to go."

"I need to go..." Lucky stood there, vibrating, nose now bleeding profusely.

"Tell that to your feet!" she snarled.

"Even Lucky Miller wants you stopped," Pipsqueak said. "He's fighting the laws of the universe itself just to stop you." Lucky looked like he was going to pass out from blood loss.

"This is not his fight," Mavis said, "this is a fight between The Thing That Makes It So and a few upstarts who stand in its way. We have no quarrel with Lucky Miller, but his luck will run out very quickly unless he gets gone!"

Emm clutched her broken moonstone necklace, then raised it to show Mavis. "You're weak, Mavis. We have enough moonstone here to finish you."

Mavis corked an eyebrow in disbelief and then sidled up to Emm, slowly. "I was like you, once. A scared, lost little girl. I knew that being a princess wasn't anything to wish for. Not like your *Norm* stepmother over there." Steph looked down at her feet and knew that Mavis was right. "She's dying to be a princess, did you know that? But you and I, Emm... we know the truth. Why be a princess when you can be a queen?"

"I'm not a queen or a princess or a fairy tale," Emm said. "I'm not a superhero or some chosen one. I'm just me. Just a person."

"And what person doesn't want to live forever? Knowledge of all the secrets of the infinite? Ultimate power over humanity? A house in the Hollywood Hills?"

"Umm, I wouldn't?"

"Enough of this," Professor Pipsqueak said under

his breath, and tossed the moonstone battle axe to Emm. Emm wrapped her necklace around the handle and all the moonstones began to glow, brighter than they had glowed before.

"You can't attack until Lucky is gone," Mavis said. "If you do, he'll be as normal and lame as your stepmother." Mavis came in closer, as though the moonstones weren't inches from her body, and told Emm a little secret: "you know Lucky is eleven hundred years old, right? He won't look nearly as hunky to you when his hair goes white or when his skin turns to dust."

Pedro the Wolf-Boy hobbled his way to one side. Loyal John to the other. The Oddities formed a circle around Mavis, ready to destroy her corporeal form once again. Olly did not look compelled to save Lucky Miller as he held his lighter beneath the nozzle of an aerosol can and waited for a signal.

"Emm, you're already so connected to the infinite," Mavis said. "I can feel it. The sun can give you anything you want. Join me."

"Just stop talking," Emm said, looking over Lucky. Lucky looked like he was going to have an aneurysm. Everyone waited for Emm's signal to attack.

Mavis did stop talking for a moment. Then she knelt a little so that Emm had to look down to see Mavis's face. Mavis's eyes seemed to soften, like Emm was looking into the eyes of a trusted old friend. "Let me tell you a little story and maybe it'll make you change your mind," Mavis said. "I grew up in the Mojave desert, in a do-nothing shanty town called Perdido – that's Spanish for lost. Just me and my mother and no money. Sound familiar? We lived in a trailer home that wasn't even ours. And when the police found out we were living there, well, my momma had to find somewhere else. We lived in abandoned cars and people's sheds, a burnt-out garage and even a cardboard box."

"Boo-hoo," Olly said, but Emm didn't hear him. She let Mavis continue.

"And then my momma went out for food one morning and she never came back. I looked everywhere... I even talked to strangers, who walked away from me like I was a monster, but I imagine that was on account of the smell and my tattered old clothes that had all gone brown from the sand. Anyway, she was gone, and I was eight, my only worldly possession was a storybook I couldn't read and my only friend in the world?" Mavis pointed skyward.

"He's always around," Mavis continued. "He keeps you warm. And if you trust him, he'll tell you his secrets. Only thing I ever wanted was that no child should live like I lived. We should all get a chance to feel pretty, and powerful, and magical, and royal. We should all get to have our wishes come true. Don't you agree? I see you do."

Emm had loosened her grip on the moonstone battleaxe and it was lowered to the floor.

57

"Don't listen to her, Emm," Steph said.

"You realize what we can do together," Mavis continued as she rose and straightened. "It's the way we should have always been." Mavis looked at Steph as she told Emm: "Let me take you under my wing, and together, we can change the world."

"Remember your home schooling!" Steph cried. "Robert Wheeler!"

"Global cooling," Emm said to herself. Then she asked Mavis, "if everything's so double-rainbow, why are you turning girls into murdering monsters?"

"You must destroy to create, my dear. These girls wanted to be princesses and now they are. They are an army of princesses who offer up their lives to help change the world. You can help us save so many lives if you would just join us. Join me. We can do amazing things together."

And throw the world into an ice age that would kill us all. War. Chaos. Famine. Hatred.

Emm looked at Steph and told Mavis: "why be amazing when normal is amazing?"

"Nothing is amazing about normal, Emm. That's why we wish for more."

"I think this is the part of the fairy tale where I slay the evil dragon."

Mavis did not take kindly to being called a dragon. "Join me, Emm," Mavis said again. "Join me or I'll kill you like I killed your father. Slow and hot."

"That's **it**." Emm let go of all her anger, all her cares, didn't think or feel at all. She just swung, with all her might, with the augmented two-handed battle axe, heaved the axe sideways into Mavis's hip, blade first, and the splash of opal milky-white light burned the clothing and flesh as it touched her, like a soldering iron through paper, and Mavis watched Emm's strike split her in two. And as her upper torso spun in mid-air, separated from her legs and almost afloat for a moment, Mavis seemed to smile. There was a sulfur and brimstone roar, which didn't come from Mavis's mouth, and another, larger flash of moonlight, and Mavis disappeared.

Lucky Miller fell to the floor.

"Guys?" Olly said, and then they all turned to see what Olly was looking at: the zombies poured into The Alcove.

"Aie dios mio," Pedro said to himself, too weary to fight anymore.

Emm tossed the axe back to Professor Pipsqueak and reached for two throwing hatchets. Pipsqueak pulled the necklace off of the handle and put the heart-shaped pendant back in her palm.

"So how do we cut the cord?" Emm asked as a tidal wave of murderous zombies rolled toward them.

Steph didn't answer. She just pulled Emm's hand and dragged her into the change room, narrowly missing the wave of zombies that would have surely killed them all. Professor Pipsqueak said good luck to them, slammed the door to the change room shut, and was overrun by twenty zombies.

58

It was eerily silent in the mirror room, and not just because their minds told them that a thousand zombies were in the room next door, screaming and killing and dying. It was sensory-deprivation quiet. That's when it occurred to Emm: *if this room never sees the sun, and it's covered in mirrors, how come there's enough light to see? Enough light to see her dad...*

She looked over at the spot where Derek Dillinger had come to her, then looked back at the circular stone couch, with the empty barrel atop it, and a tiara sitting there, glowing so glamorously, waiting for a victim to try it on and grow tarnished.

"We need to destroy this place and lock Mavis out of our world," Steph said, just about ready to lay a dropkick on a mirror.

"I saw Dad in here, you know," Emm said. Steph froze. "He came to me when I put the tiara on. In the reflection."

Steph touched the glass. Then she looked back at the tiara shining in the center of the room and wanted to put it on more than ever. "Impossible..." Steph whispered to herself.

"If we destroy this place, will we ever see Dad again?"

Steph took a couple of steps over to the circular stone couch. "I don't know. I don't know what it means. You can't bring back the dead." *But maybe I can bring him back if I become a princess. I always wanted to be a princess... didn't I?*

"I didn't bring him back. He just came for a visit... 'be pure of heart and remember where magic lives.' He told me to tell you that."

That broke Steph's focus on the crown. She looked into her girl's eyes. *Remember where magic lives.* "Maybe you saw Derek and maybe it was a trick. The plan is to destroy the shortcut and that's what we have to do."

"The plan... you forced me to go to school, just so I could be part of this plan, didn't you?"

Steph stepped back. "We needed you, Emm. We tried to get you ready. Professor Pipsqueak had been following Mavis for a couple of years, and when she opened Spindle, we knew that it was time for you to lead us. It had to be you." Steph sat on the couch and looked into Emm's eyes. "But you weren't ready. I couldn't just throw you to the wolves. So I sent you to school, got Professor Pipsqueak to watch over you. And then things moved way too fast."

Emm looked at her stepmother with a face Steph couldn't quite read. Anger? Suspicion? Torment? "You. You never wanted me to be normal," Emm said. "I never had a chance."

Steph shook her head. Emm was right. She never did have a chance to be a regular kid. Steph looked away, but all she saw was her own reflection and she was so ashamed of it, she looked back at Emm. *I'm so ashamed of being normal and yet it's the only thing Emm ever wanted.*

But, to Steph's surprise, Emm's expression had melted into warm, heartened smile. "Best. Mom. Ever." Emm said.

I don't deserve this kid, Steph thought, then she sniffed and tried to reel in the tears. Emm came up to her and gave her a hug. "I'm sure," Steph sniffled, "that there will be other ways a magical kid like you will be able to see her crazy wizard ghost dad."

"Come on," Emm said. "I'm sick of looking at myself."

They held hands, counted to three, and kicked as hard as they could. The mirror smashed, but instead of bricks or stone or walls, the mirror shards fell away to reveal red volcanic light, just like what they saw beneath the floor of the Jacob Williams High School gymnasium. It seemed to breathe as they broke more and more mirror, heaving itself up into a white glow, then cooling down to orange and red, then back to white.

Bye, Dad, Emm thought as she kicked and pounded the spot where they had spoken. As they went lower and lower, the reflective surface became more and more difficult to break, until they got to the floor, which withstood their hardest kicks. Emm looked for something to break it with, but the only thing she could think of to try was the tiara. She took the diamond point at the fore of the tiara and pressed it into the mirror. It etched the glass, just like a spy who cuts a stealthy hole into a window so they can sneak inside. Emm made a shape.

"What are you doing?" Steph said. Emm swerved, obviously not making a circle. "Are you making... a butt?!?"

Emm stopped etching. "Hello, it's a heart? Jeez," and she finished. The heart-shaped cut in the mirror popped up a hair's width from the floor, and Emm needed to pry it up with the tiara. Wind blew fiercely from the hole, but Emm continued. Steph was standing so far away, Emm needed to say "a little help, here?" so they could lift the heart off of the floor. It made a pleasing smash as it flipped onto its backside and exploded into a million bits.

59

The heart-shaped hole it left wasn't the same as the holes in the walls; it was as though the change room was suspended above another world, with nothing to keep Emm from just falling down a mile into the flames and red rock and embers of the world below them; the place to which this change room was a short cut.

"There it is," Steph said. "It's awful." It rippled with heat and electromagnetic tempests, like the surface of the sun itself. Or some other fiery place.

"So the T T M I S lives there?" Emm said. Steph looked at her blankly. "Thing That Makes It So?"

"Emm..." Steph said as she spied something below.

"Ya?"

"Time to go now." Steph pointed. A figure was taking shape in the flames. A perfect ass and perfectly straight hair. Mavis. Except Mavis was now a thousand feet tall. Mavis rumbled as the flames formed her face. The face looked up at them.

"Necklace," Steph said. *I love you, Emm.* Emm handed her the necklace. Steph rushed to the wall where they had come in; the wall was now embers and there was still no crack to pry open.

"Help us!" Steph screamed.

"Hey! We're ready to come out now!" Emm screamed.

The floor began to fall away from the heart-shaped hole, leaving less and less floor to stand on. The circular stone couch dropped like a spaceship re-entering the atmosphere, flaming up and then glowing white-hot as it neared the surface. A tremor rose up like an earthquake, a vibration so deep they didn't recognize it to be Mavis's voice for a full second.

"I'm coming," the tremors said at a wavelength no human voice could achieve. More of the walls shattered.

Steph stood with the necklace gripped tightly in her hand, staring fearlessly at the fires below.

Emm pounded even harder on the wall. "Please!" Emm shouted. She could see Mavis's flaming hand, the size of a jumbo jet, reaching up. Reaching for them. A maelstrom of swirling whirlwinds became so strong that Steph and Emm could barely stay upright.

Finally, the door opened. Emm looked over at Steph, but Steph was looking at Mavis. Emm couldn't be sure, and perhaps it would be something that would haunt Emm for the rest of her life, but Steph seemed to relax for a moment. Just long enough for the swirling winds to pick her up and sweep her to the edge of the precipice over the flaming world and Mavis's flaming reach. It could have been accidental, but it looked to Emm like it was on purpose.

That was the first part of Emm's last memory of Steph.

Steph was on her belly when she yelled "We can't let her get out. Go!" and held up Emm's necklace. Emm dove through the door, but immediately turned and looked back at Steph.

Emm fell to her knees and reached for Steph, imploring her to take her hand. Steph looked Emm right in the eye and began to reach up.

That's when Steph uttered her last words. She pushed Emm's hand away. "You're ready now," Steph said, and reached for the door. The flaming jumbo jet-sized hand grabbed her at the exact same time as Steph slammed the door shut.

A moonstone flash of milky white light seeped through the tiniest, invisible seam in the door. And then there was nothing. Emm pounded on the door and screamed louder than she ever had before, but it was no use.

Steph wasn't there anymore.

60

Emm wasn't sure how long she had pounded her fists against the door that wouldn't open anymore, but it was Olly's voice that finally got her to stop. She turned and slumped against the wall, and that's when she saw the two hundred zombie corpses piled up in the middle of The Alcove. Pedro the Wolf-Boy and Loyal John, Professor Pipsqueak and Olly the Sperminator, all covered in blood, wounded and exhausted, slumped against other walls.

Olly wheeled himself to the head of a zombie princess and picked up her tiara.

It turned to ash and fell through his fingers.

"You did it," he said, with no smile or excitement. He was too exhausted.

"We won, child," Professor Pipsqueak said.

"But my mom..."

"She upheld... her oath," Pedro said through a bloody mouth. "We all have today..." His eyes shut and very nearly didn't reopen. "An Oddity fights to the death to stay Odd."

"To the death," Pipsqueak chimed. "She was a brave woman. She was one of us by choice. Nothing freakish about her, that any of us ever knew."

"So not true," Emm sniffled. "Steph was a Devastating Dillinger of Doom. If she didn't spin on the wheel, we had no act. If she didn't train me to throw the hatchets, we'd all be dead. If she didn't teach me how to read and do math, and make me pb & j's, well, I guess I'd be dead, too. So I say Steph was a freak, just like us. She had a freakishly ginormous heart."

"Perhaps that is something we all wished we had."

"Guys," John said, "I know we're happy that we won and stuff, but look." He showed them his metal hand. "Still metal."

"We vanquished Mavis," Professor Pipsqueak said, "but the will of the universe lives on. The wishes of the human heart live on. Fairy tales live on."

"So do zombies," Olly said.

"So do zombies, someplace," Professor Pipsqueak agreed. "So do all the fantasies of the Norms. The Norms still need saving, Emm. Will you help us save them?"

Emm looked into Olly's eyes and thought about all the heartbreak she's already caused him. And how he would never walk again. How he had died and she had brought him back to life with a single kiss.

She looked at Loyal John's square face, so strong and resolute, but so sad. The sacrifices he already made, just to uphold his vows. Just to be loyal.

Pedro, so old and frail, another soldier nearing the end of his time.

Professor Pipsqueak. Maybe the strongest and bravest of all the Oddities.

And then she looked back at the door to the room that took Steph away, forgot about the question, and cried for her stepmother.

61

Once upon a time, the sun was given a mirror. It wasn't uncommon for a star to have a mirror so it could see its own reflection and embrace its vanity; in fact, moons littered the cosmos, each of them reflecting a star or even two stars at once, casting an eerie light onto the atmospheres of the planets they orbited.

Well, if you think a teenaged girl with a princess complex can be vain, give that girl the ability to shape the universe in her own image and see where that gets you. Being vain, the sun despises its own reflection, is never for a nanosecond satisfied with it, and that is why moonstone keeps The Thing That Makes It So at bay.

Moonstone isn't from the moon. At least not the moon that spins around our home. No, no. But moonstone possesses the same reflective quality, crystallized and concentrated to such a degree that the fires of The Thing retreat in horror when it senses the presence of moonstone. Its holy whiteness, in its creamy tranquil glory, can reach out and touch the most fiery of us and cool us into ice. It is something to behold if you ever get the chance.

My… relatives (I wouldn't call them ancestors, because I am merely human, Odd though I may be) were a group of miners who discovered moonstone, deep beneath the surface of the Earth. It didn't take them long to discover the protective qualities of moonstone and they used it to protect a certain princess from the clutches of an untrustworthy prince, with whom they had had previous mercantile dealings.

At any rate, moonstone behaves well, but it's not entirely predictable. Especially when it is used in abundance. So take great care, human with moonstone earrings, for thou knowest not what jiggles in thine earlobes.

In summation, rubes, ruffians and rabble:

A) **The Thing That Makes It So is fire.**
B) **The fire is conscious.**
C) **We govern the fire with our wishes.**
D) **Moonstone can keep the fire at bay.**
E) **The Oddities are mankind's only chance against another cosmic reboot.**

The least you could do is applaud when I stick a perfect telemark landing from the trapeze. It's twice as far down for me, you know.

—*another unheard lecture from Professor Pipsqueak, recounted here verbatim*

62

Steph cried for her stepdaughter as she fell to the flames of The Thing That Makes It So. There was an easy way for Steph to survive, she thought: have a couple of hundred thousand people wish she would come back, all at the same time. If it was physically possible, that would get her right out of this mess. As long as she wasn't dead already. It was a distinct possibility that she was dead already.

The conduit to Earth was destroyed the moment Steph slammed the door shut, and Mavis might have been destroyed as well, since her giant hand vanished when the door slammed shut. The moonstone necklace, which Derek had put around Emm's neck long before Steph had ever met them, exploded as soon as the door shut, too, blinding Steph and leaving her empty-handed as she began her fall.

That was fifteen minutes ago.

Steph was starting to wonder if she was ever going to land. She wondered if she would fall forever now, if this was the afterlife. Just falling. What a pain in the butt that would be. She didn't feel any hotter, either, even though the flames of what she assumed was The Thing seemed to be getting closer and closer. There was no air here, and no wind resistance, so it was nothing like jumping out of an airplane or riding a motorcycle. There was a feeling of gravity, though. The sensation of falling didn't make Steph feel very well, and that queasiness was starting to get so strong that it trumped the sensation of falling. She decided to take her mind off of it; otherwise she could be dying and vomiting at the same time, and that could last for hours at this rate, or even eternity. *Might as well think about something else.*

She had been wondering whether or not Derek would be with Daphne on the other side, in the land of the dead. Steph wondered how all of that would work: would they be some kind of threesome? Was that normal in the afterlife this day and age? Was it one big love-fest? Steph wondered how she would fit in there.

And that got her thinking about the day she met Derek Dillinger, and his wife, Daphne.

Steph was a nurse in Springfield, Massachusetts fifteen years ago. She was on a date with Doctor Ron – the doctor every nurse wanted to date – and she was feeling mighty proud when he picked her up from her apartment at eight. Promptly at eight. Always a good sign.

Not such a good sign: Doctor Ron took her to see a bunch of sideshow freaks before dinner. Browning's Traveling Oddities, they were called, although there was no sign of who Browning was. Steph didn't know who Browning was to this day.

Steph was amazed by what she saw. It was like she had been transported back a hundred years: there was a hairy man who they called Pedro the Wolf-Boy; there was a midget who babbled incessantly while performing aerial hijinx; there was a set of twin contortionists, one male, one female, that could fold themselves into each other like yin and yang and bounce like a beach ball; there was a man who was so thin he could fit under a crack in the door; there was a juggler who Steph couldn't pay attention to because Doctor Ron seemed intent on feeling her leg beneath the hem of her skirt; there was a fortuneteller with a baby and she seemed to read Steph's mind better than anyone else's mind. As Doctor Ron reached over and touched Steph's inner thigh, very creepily, the fortuneteller rose from six rows away and moved to them, glaring into the doctor's hazel eyes. "Get out," the fortuneteller said. The baby began to cry. "Get out, get out!" And Doctor Ron scrambled off, to the unsettled din of the crowd.

"Don't get up," the fortuneteller told Steph, just as every fibre in Steph's being told her to get up and leave, too. Then the fortuneteller seemed to drop her mask for a moment, like she forgot to act like a sideshow fortuneteller. "Please, don't get up," the lady said. The baby looked into Steph's eyes and stopped crying. It was as though the baby recognized her.

Steph was royally freaked out. The fortuneteller rested her hand on Steph's and whispered "Stay" before skitting off behind a curtain, to a smattering of polite applause.

The main attraction was a magician – The Amazing Dillinger, the carnival barker barked. Dillinger came in with his smoky good looks and fedora tipped to the side, performed a couple of very clichéd sleights of hand, and then asked for a volunteer from the audience.

Steph was certain she hadn't raised her hand. She was sure of it. She even told herself *do not raise your hand, get out of this tent right now, this is super creepy and you need to leave.* But she had stayed in her seat. And when The Amazing Dillinger pointed at Steph, and said "you," Steph went to point at herself and say "me?" but realized her hand was too busy being raised. With nothing left to do, she got up and walked to the center of the stage, to a smattering of polite applause.

As she got closer, Derek gave her a furtive little smile that only she could see. Then he turned to the audience, flourished with his arms, and... stopped dead in his tracks. As though he was getting a transmission in his ear from the Mothership.

"Uh, I'm sorry, Miss..." he said, and then he abruptly left the stage. Steph just stood there, in the middle of the stage, with the entire crowd staring dumbly at her. The carnival barker came back into the tent. "Show's over, folks. Medical emergency. Is there a doctor in the house? How about a nurse?"

Steph was brought backstage, through the curtain, and she never returned from behind it.

Now she would never see the stage again.

63

Emm continued to bawl her eyes out, waiting outside the change room door for Steph to somehow open that door and come back. Emm would have traded the world to get Steph back. She would have let the world go to zombie princess hell to get Steph back.

She would have stayed like that forever, like a curled-up statue with a fountain of perpetual tears, but a strange noise filled her ears. It sounded like... vacuuming?

It *was* vacuuming. At the entrance to Spindle, past the rubble and the carnage in The Alcove, Emm could see a squadron of men in white hazmat suits and tinted masks. They were headed to The Alcove. Emm reached for her throwing hatchets, but Professor Pipsqueak rested a hand on her shoulder.

"Don't fret," he said to her. "That's just the cleanup crew."

Cleanup crew?

Professor Pipsqueak chortled. "You didn't think we'd just leave all these poor people and all this horror where they could be found, did you? Did you think we'd call CNN to brag?"

Two men in hazmat suits worked together to bring in a long, tubular object: a vacuum. The roaring sound got louder as they vacuumed up everything: bodies, broken glass, magical fairy tale artifacts, all of it.

Olly sat a little ahead of Emm and she could see the back of his head as it cocked to one side, curiously looking at the clean-up crew in white. Six of them entered The Alcove, one with a clipboard. He seemed to be taking some kind of inventory, obviously being able to see through the reflective facemask that shielded his or her face. Handling a pen with gloves that thick must take some practice, Olly thought to himself. The clipboard guy pointed at some bodies and the others started picking through the corpses. After a minute, one gave an astronaut-gloved thumbs-up to the clipboard guy and the giant vacuum came whining in to suck up all the gore.

Olly, John and Pedro didn't seem too startled at the intrusion of this clean-up crew. *Are we going to all get vacuumed up too, someday?* Emm thought. And then something else occurred to her. She looked up at Professor Pipsqueak with a suspicious look.

"If I'm going to join 'us', you're going to have to explain who, exactly, we are."

64

Lucky Miller had a dream. In that dream, the Thing That Makes It So spoke to him. This wasn't all that uncommon; in order for Lucky to do the Thing's bidding, there needed to be some instruction. This was the way that Lucky received those marching orders: dreams where the The Thing That Makes It So spoke to him.

But something was different about this dream. There was someone else there, and it wasn't the King, who continued to paddle the ferry across the river, delivering "souls" to "Hell" (Lucky knew that this was all metaphor and short-hand for simplistic human brains to comprehend the connecting between destruction and creation, hence the quotes). No, someone else emerged from the shadow of Lucky's dream, and she wore a crown. She was royalty... familiar royalty. *Where have I seen that face before?*

What's the diff, she's pretty, I'll have myself a big slice of that. And in Lucky's dream, he walked closer to the girl with the crown, with the hair as black as pitch, and lips as red as blood, and skin as white as snow.

That earth-rattling rumble... was that a laugh? It distracted Lucky for a moment. And then the message from Thing came into his dream, loud and clear: marry the princess and the fates forsake you. Your wedding day approaches.

And then Lucky was struck with a lightning bolt of recognition: the princess was Emm Dillinger.

He had been tricked. Fallen in lust with the one who could end it all. A little bait-and-switch. A little shell game. Didn't even occur to Lucky that The Thing That Makes It So might have been sending Lucky a princess to marry, since there were so many tiaras and the world looked as though it might end. Now, Lucky thought, his days of immortal good fortune were about to end.

He awoke.

Lucky's ill-fated battle of wills against Mavis ended with him left unconscious on the floor of The Alcove, where he would surely have been trampled, but it just so happened that every rampaging zombie stepped a little to the left, or a little to the right, and Lucky lay there untouched after all the carnage. The Oddities were too busy fighting for their own hides to notice his body jostling around in the mass melee, getting covered in blood and guts. So when Lucky came to, he wiped blood from his eyes and believed it to be his own. He was mortal, just as Mavis had threatened. He was going to die.

As he sat up and slid his fingers across his cheeks to squeegee the blood off, he realized he wasn't in The Alcove anymore. He wasn't in the shopping mall. He knew where he was, and because of that, Lucky Miller had no clue where in the heck he had ended up.

Lucky got to his feet, pulled out his pack of Lucky Strikes, pulled out the last bent-up cigarette. He rolled it a little to straighten it out and then lit it.

He looked around the flour mill, still in disbelief

that it was indeed the place of his birth and the place of his childhood. Lucky had seen the place burn to the ground after he had left it; he was certain it had been incinerated more than a thousand years ago. Yet, here it was. *One way to verify,* Lucky thought. He headed for his old bedroom, calling out hello as he went, but there was no reply. He looked out the window as he went up the staircase. A herd of cows from the nieghbour's pasture, as though he they had never stopped munching on his family's grass. Son of a mother.

His bed was exactly as he had left it. Lucky paused for a moment, welling up with nostalgia, and thought about spreading his hands across the bed and pressing his cheek against the sheets he had slept on for seventeen years. Instead, as he lowered to his knees, he pulled the bedframe so that it slid away from the wall, and then dove on the bed – its spring exactly the same as it was a thousand years ago – and reached over the other side, to the floorboards. He stuck a fingernail between two floorboards and, sure enough, one popped open with ease, just as it did. He popped up the next one, and the next. There was no doubt now – Lucky was convinced he had travelled back eleven centuries, and soon he would pull out the ring his parents had given him to betroth himself to the Princess, as his markings foretold.

The markings! He looked on his wrist: *gone.* He rolled onto his back and feverishly rolled up his blood-soaked pantleg. *Gone.* He pulled his collar out as far as it would go and peered down at his breastbone. *Gone! I'm mortal! Mavis stole my good fortune from me!*

Unsure of what to do next, Lucky Miller puffed the last puff of his cigarette as he sat on the bed, then thought about quitting, since he would surely die of cancer now. Also it would be difficult to buy Lucky Strikes in the twelfth century. Panic subsided and now he just felt dejected. *It was a fun millennium-plus,* he thought. Then he very carefully butted his cigarette out under the sole of his shoe.

When he decided to fish out the ring from its hiding place beneath the floorboards of his bedroom, Lucky made a discovery that changed everything, and yet changed nothing.

There was no ring beneath the floorboards. He had reached down, felt some jewelry, and pulled it out to inspect, and there, dangling in his freckled, tobacco-yellowed fingers, was Emm Dillinger's heart-shaped moonstone necklace.

65

Sun Gorge, Wisconsin had a high school, but it wasn't a tenth the size of the former Jacob Williams High School. So on her first day, Emm wasn't exactly vibrating, and she didn't feel compelled to stare down at her black Mary Janes. All the same, she was still apprehensive.

"I don't really know if school is for me, you know?" She told the guidance counselor. "I mean, the pressure to fit in... the competition to be the prettiest and the smartest... I just don't know if I can do it."

Mr. Blake looked up from the mountain of paperwork on his desk and offered Emm a warm smile.

"Somehow, I think you'll do fine here," Mr. Blake said.

"Now then," Mr. Blake said. "I've had three kids report sightings of a thumb-sized boy running across the schoolyard this week..."

The schoolyard had an ancient, rusted-out old swing set, and Emm sat in it all afternoon, skipping all of her classes, though Mr. Blake had already tutored her through so many credits that she could have graduated the previous semester. But graduating kind of defeated the purpose of working undercover in a high school.

Finally, beside a soccer goalpost about fifty yards away,

Emm spied a movement in the bare grass. Could have been a field mouse, could have been a feather blowing in the breeze. Emm was pretty sure it was Tom Thumb. She hopped off of the swing and crept up to the goalpost as quietly as she could. She saw another movement from about thirty yards away and knew it wasn't a feather... twenty yards... ten yards... and a blonde-haired boy the size of a human digit came dancing out from behind the goalpost, really boogieing, and Emm spied two tiny white wires going up to his ears. He was wearing a teensy tiny iPod. Emm snickered at the cutesy little guy, and the snicker alerted the thumb-sized boy to Emm's presence.

The boy screamed blue murder and ran for the farmer's field, just outside the schoolyard.

"Help! Help!" The boy screamed, though it sounded like a robin's chirp.

"Wait!" Emm said, "I won't hurt you!" She could easily outrun him if she dropped her backpack and the hatchets she had tucked away in there, so she dropped it in the middle of the field and lunged for him. She tried to scoop him up, but the little guy was elusive. He would bound through her hand, then barrel-roll and juke with each swipe. He even vaulted up as she leaned down and then he landed on the back of her shirt and held on for dear life as she rose back up. Emm stopped and searched around, completely clueless that he was hanging from her back. Instinctively, she swatted at the back of her neck when she felt a mosquito itch. *Oh no!* She pulled her hand away and showed it to herself, fully expecting there to be thumb-sized boy guts all over her palm. She opened her hand. Nothing.

Then she saw some blades of grass parting just ahead. Chase back on.

Emm got to the farmer's field, where barley grew tall and thick, and stopped. She knew she'd never find him in there, and he must have known that too.

"Don't be afraid!" Emm shouted. "We just want to talk to you!"

No response. Total silence for a moment. Total stillness. And then, a single stalk of barley twinged just a bit. Emm dashed for it, and that made several stalks of barley move, and then Emm noticed a bald patch ahead where no barley grew. She started to hear birds chirping. She got to the clearing and immediately realized that what she heard was, in fact, not the chirping of birds.

It was the sound of ninety seven thumb-sized people having a very panicked conversation. They screamed and ran in all different directions as Emm gasped. She realized she must have looked like Godzilla to them. Emm backed away and said "sorry, sorry," as if she had just walked in on somebody going to the bathroom.

A voice from behind her made Emm spin around. The voice boomed, proudly and clearly, and it most certainly did not belong to a person the size of a thumb.

"Thank you, fair damsel, for your top-notch sleuthery," said a familiar voice.

Emm immediately forgot about the tiniest town hall she had just interrupted as she looked up, up and up at three young men, muscular square-jawed, wearing epaulets on their skin-tight outfits. Their capes were bright red, bright yellow, and royal blue. And they descended from their superhero flight slowly and heroically. The biggest one, who must have been the leader, had black shiny hair and a little curlicue on the forehead. He was the one who had thanked Emm for her top-notch sleuthery.

"You have uncovered the enclave of a secret society of evil," he continued. He sounded like Dudley Do-Right. (Emm had been watching old cartoons and found them to be much more amusing than Glee).

"Who are you?" Emm said.

"We are the League of Justified Vengeance," he declared. The other two seemed to puff their chests out a little bit. "I am SuperCharming, that is Charming Man, and the other is Night Charming. Now aid us in our quest to rid the world of evil, or prepare to die!"

A silver fist emerged from the barley field. It hit SuperCharming square on the jaw and set the superfairyhero reeling. John stumbled out of from the bushes and SuperCharming turned to battle him – with red eyebeams that set crops on fire. John used his metal hand to shield himself from the ray.

The one in the royal blue – must have been Night Charming – looked down at his own chest. A metal spike poked out from it. A flash of white light as Night Charming became frentrails that fell to the soil, Emm saw Olly's face, the bearer of the metal spike. Olly hovered above the ground, strapped into his newfangled hoverpack.

"We got this," Olly said to her as he spit out a little bit of frog parts. It was very heroic-sounding. Olly's heart didn't hurt one bit in its cage.

The third super-powered Prince Charming – *Charming Man? Really?* – saw the green bits that used to be Night Charming and flew into the sky, his knee raised and fist skyward in true stereotypical superhero fashion.

"We were trailing these three... they got some kind of signal to come here," John said as he struggled against the laser-eyes.

"And now our job is done here," SuperCharming said as he closed his eyes and the red eyebeam stopped. Barley was on fire everywhere. The thumb-sized people were long gone. "Sun Gorge is now safe, thanks to the League of Justified Vengeance!" SuperCharming said as he flew away, just like his fellow League of Justified Vengeance person had flown away – knee up, fist skyward. His black curlicue flapping in the air heroically.

"We just got rickrolled," Olly said as they watched SuperCharming fly away.

"What?" John said as he got to his feet.

"I have a bad feeling about this," Emm said, as she wondered what had just happened to the rest of Sun Gorge, Wisconsin.

End of BOOK ONE

The Oddities, book two

LEAGUE of JUSTIFIED VENGEANCE

Coming in 2012

www.zombieprincessapocalypse.com